THE WITCH'S DETECTIVE

KAREN THROWER

This is a work of fiction. Names, characters, places, and incidents are products of the author's imagination or are used fictitiously and are not to be construed as real. Any resemblance to actual events, locations, organizations, or persons, living or dead, is entirely coincidental.

World Castle Publishing, LLC
Pensacola, Florida

Copyright © 2024 Karen Thrower
Hardcover ISBN: 9798323005451
Paperback ISBN: 9798891261976
eBook ISBN: 9798891261983
First Edition World Castle Publishing, LLC, May 21, 2024
http://www.worldcastlepublishing.com

Licensing Notes

Cover: Cover Designs by Karen
Cover-designs-by-karen.com
Editor: Karen Fuller

CHAPTER ONE

My name is Lily Roa, and I am a witch. I use my powers to help the local police officers with their more… unusual cases. We all grew up with magic, faeries, and monsters, but not everyone is equipped to handle them. There's always a great deal of intolerance against the magical community. Whether it stems from fear or jealousy, it's not likely to go away anytime soon. So I'm like a bridge between the two.

The police are great for human crimes, but when it comes to the preternatural, I get called in. There's nothing like proving a creature is innocent when there's a lynch mob after it. Or helping the police find the true creature responsible. Humans tend to struggle with the unknown, and I don't blame us. The world is scary at times. But in the end, I want to make sure we all end up on the same side.

"Uuurrrp." I sighed in relief. A mighty burp

was exactly what I needed. I had two more slices of pizza I wanted to eat. The delivery guy didn't believe little ol' me could eat an entire pizza, but clearly, he underestimated the cravings of one suffering from PMS. Teenagers aren't the only ones who can pack it away.

I stretched on the couch and scratched my stomach. I hadn't had a night off in two weeks, with working as a consultant for the Arion police department or cleansing a house every other night. I almost forgot how to relax, so I decided to watch some movies. I recently read an article about the best horror movies currently streaming, and as I browsed through about a hundred of them online, my cell phone rang.

I groaned and swiped right. "Yeah?"

"Ms. Roa?" *Crap, there goes my relaxing night.* No one called me 'Ms.Roa' except the police.

"That's me."

"Ms.Roa, my name is Detective Moss. I'm with the Arion Police department. Captain Howard Adams gave me your number." Howard was the one who called me when the police needed my unique services at a crime scene. Typically, I got a call from him at least once a week, but lately, it seemed like every other day. Arion seemed to be in the middle of a flap of high strangeness at the moment. Fine with me if it meant more money in my pocket.

"Ah, Howard, thank you so much," I picked up one of the pizza slices and took a bite. "What can I do for you, Detective?"

"There's been a murder, and we need a w...uh, someone with your expertise."

I swallowed my bite. "It's okay, you can say it," I took another bite and managed to talk around it. "It's not a bad word, I promise, you need a...."

He cleared his throat. "Witch."

"There ya go!" I set my slice down and clapped for him. "See, that's not so hard. Now, why call me? I'm not the only witch in town. The Fell's are also on retainer." I often wondered what it might be like being in a magical relationship like the Fells. Would it be beneficial or a hindrance? I shouldn't wonder too much about it. I don't even have a boyfriend. It'd be a while before I had another one. Not many people moved to Arion, and there's no way a local would date me. Which is fine. They're all jerks because they think I killed my family.

"I might be super busy. As a matter-of-fact Detective, I was just about to watch," I looked at the TV screen and picked the first title I saw. "Satan's tongue, ew what? No! Who comes up with that crap?"

I thought I heard a snicker over the line. "Yeah, we tried them," Moss said, "Apparently, they're on vacation and won't be back until tomorrow." I cursed internally. I forgot Jackson and Amelia went to Cancun.

I sighed and rolled my eyes. "I forgot. Text me the address, I'll be there within the hour."

"Sorry to pull you away from the scariest movie of the year," I saw that was the tagline of the movie. "See you soon, Ms. Roa." I swiped left and got to my feet. Thankfully, I didn't spill any pizza sauce on my shirt. I just had to brush the parmesan and garlic dust off, throw some pants on, and I'd be ready. I was going to a murder scene. Makeup wasn't required.

***

I got in my little white car and typed the address into the GPS. Seems the murder happened a few blocks away from my apartment. I hate it when serious stuff happens close to where I live. I can't help but wonder if there had been anything I could have done to prevent it. But witch or no, I was only human, and I couldn't stop every terrible thing that happened in my town. I pulled an extra hair band off my visor and quickly tried to tame my dark, curly hair. I had my mother to thank for my bountiful coif. Thick, curly hair was dominant on my mother's side, and I could believe it. My Abuela was in her sixties when she died, and her hair had no signs of thinning. Having your hair pulled back at a murder scene can keep you from accidentally getting blood in it, as well. You only make that mistake once, so that was my usual hairdo at these kinds of things.

After a few blocks, I turned one last right and saw police cars and ambulances down the street. The houses were mostly cute cape cod style, with perfectly manicured lawns and seasonally appropriate flowers planted, so lots of oranges and yellows for the fall. Not the usual background for a murder investigation in our town. Don't get me wrong, all towns have crime, but ours usually happens in the back alleys and the south side of town, not in the idyllic neighborhoods that were put on the travel brochures. I pulled over a few houses away from the crime scene tape and got out. I could feel magic waver through the air, and the hair on my arms stood up. That usually meant dark magic had been used or something dark had been there. Believe it or not, there was a difference. There was also a pull, like something wanted me there. That made me nervous.

I ducked under the tape, flashing my ID to the rookies guarding the yellow line, and they backed off. Most of the older guys knew me from work or having lived in the town their entire life, but occasionally, I had to put an out-of-town newbie in his place.

I walked up to the sergeant on duty. "A Detective Moss called me," I couldn't remember the sergeant's name, Doug? I looked at his name tag, Dougal, that's right. Close enough.

He turned around and yelled towards the

houses. "Moss! Your witch is here."

"So, what have we got?" From my vantage, all I could see were cars and ambulances. Everything must have still been inside one of the houses. Dougal shifted. He looked almost nervous as his thumbs hooked under his vest at his chest.

"Homicide, multiple bodies, human, fey, something else." I noticed he wouldn't look at me. That wasn't unusual, but with his nervous demeanor, it made me wary.

I crossed my arms and tried not to take offense. "Is the something else the murderer?"

He grimaced. "No, I think it was a pet or something. Some weird fey creature." *Ahh, my specialty, weird, fey things*. I rolled my eyes at his indifference.

"Well magic was definitely involved, I could feel it by my car."

He cleared his throat. "Yeah, I'll take your word for it." Something in his voice made me pause. There wasn't the usual annoyance or loathing, he almost sounded…sad.

"Dougal, what is it?"

But he ignored me. "That's Moss." Dougal pointed off to his left and walked off. I turned and saw a man in a suit and tie come jogging over. He looked like he was in his early thirties and had a handsome face.

I let the detective finish his jog and held my hand out when he reached me. "Moss?"

He shook my hand, nice and firm, good. Nothing worse than a limp handshake. Maybe a sweaty one. Ugh.

"Yeah, that's me. You must be Ms.Roa."

"I am. You can call me Lily."

He motioned with his head to a house on the north side of the street. "If you'll follow me, I'll show you the crime scene." I nodded and followed. The house was white with dark colored shutters, green maybe? It was hard to tell at night with the constant flicker of all the emergency vehicles. There was also a dark colored SUV in the driveway, and it caught my eye. *Do I know that car?* I wondered, trying to ignore the pull that came from inside the house, a pull that told me I did. But since I couldn't immediately place the car, it was easier to ignore what my guts were telling me.

"So, when did Howard give you my number?"

"Last week," he turned to me as we walked to the house, "he said I might like working with you." I had never met Det. Moss before, but as he talked, I noticed his eyes. There was sadness in them, and I stopped him with a hand on his arm.

"Moss, what is going on? First, Dougal didn't insult me. Now you look like you have bad news."

He sighed and stepped closer to me as he leaned down. "You know one of the deceased." I held in my gasp. The pull. They had recognized me and wanted me to find them. I started to put two and two together. The vehicle I vaguely recognized, Moss called instead of Howard, and no one was giving me grief.

"Howard."

Moss laid a hand on my shoulder and nodded. "I'm sorry." I took a deep breath and faced the door. This was going to be hard.

I walked up to the door, Moss behind me, as another officer gave us gloves and booties to cover our shoes. "Now I have to warn you, it's pretty horrible," Moss sighed.

The pull was coming from the back of the house so strongly I could have sworn someone was pulling my hand towards it. The further in we got, the more insistent it became. So I walked slowly, letting it lead me.

"Dougal said Human, fey, and something else? A pet?"

"Most likely." I took a deep breath as we passed the dining room. It seemed like spaghetti and salad were for dinner. Unfortunately, it was tinged with the familiar metallic smell of blood. The dining table was off to the right and was still set perfectly, except for the one wine glass on its side, the contents staining the white tablecloth red. I walked through a door into the back bedroom and saw police officers slowly walking around, taking pictures and notes. One thing all cops learn is how to keep a blank face, but there were quite a few who weren't even trying.

Upset faces walked around me, talked quietly in corners, and were leaning against the wall, looking at the ground. I wasn't surprised. It was hard when another officer was killed. The first thing I noticed in the room was this pet everyone was talking about. It was on its side by the end of the king-sized bed, and I could tell its fur was supposed to be white, but it was covered in bloody polka dots of varying sizes. The animal was about the size of a Yorkshire terrier and had two horns sticking out of its head that looked like they had been ground down on purpose.

"First," I said, pointing at the dead creature, "this is a puca. Fey sometimes have them as pets." A few of the officers began writing what I said. It made me feel a little better. It showed they were listening to me. I took a deep breath and finally looked at the rest of the crime scene. The room was large, there were sitting chairs and bookcases filled with books and a large television on the wall opposite the bed. They all seemed untouched by the butchery. I took another breath, then looked at the bodies. It took a while for my eyes to adjust to the carnage, but through the blood-soaked carpet and strangely positioned bodies, I finally saw him. Howard. "Oh, Howard." I knew he lived nearby, but he liked to keep his work and private life separate, so I never visited. I didn't blame him. It's hard when work follows you home. Sometimes, the ghosts wanted more attention from me than I could give at a crime scene, and I ended up with an incorporeal roommate for a week.

I slowly walked over to his body and kneeled by his hand, careful not to dunk my knee in a puddle of blood. He was on his back, his legs were at odd angles, and his eyes stared at the ceiling. There was a hole in his chest, and in this world, that meant one thing. His heart was missing.

"Hey, Lil." Howard's voice made my ear twitch, and I looked up. His ghost was standing by his head, and he looked sad.

"Hey, Howard," I said, not caring who heard me speaking to something they couldn't see.

He sighed and kneeled by his body. "What a mess."

"Do you remember what happened?" I could feel the other officers staring at me. It happened every time the ghost of a victim showed up. But instead of their usual 'go about their business' attitude, the room quieted, and I knew everyone was listening intently to me.

"No." He shook his head and looked down. "Ooh, my Thicket." His translucent hand petted the white-blonde hair of the elf on the floor. Her face was buried in the carpet, blood had spread from her torso, but since no one had moved her body, it was unclear how she was murdered. But I had a feeling her heart was also missing.

"I didn't know you hung around elves, Howard."

"I tried to keep that part of myself separate from work. Thicket was my wife."

I gasped. "Your wife?"

"Wife?" Detective Moss kneeled next to me. "Did you say, wife?"

"Yeah, her name is Thicket. She was married to Howard." I looked up, and his ghost was gone. I wasn't sure if I'd see him again. Ghosts tended to come and go at will until their murders were solved. Good motivation if you ask me.

"I didn't think elves married humans," Moss said.

"Me either. He said he kept it a secret. They both did." I stood up, and a few of the officers walked over. I noticed they were all ones who didn't particularly like me for what I was.

"Did you see him?" Officer Gray asked. There was a kindness or sadness in his voice that I'd never heard in the six years I have known him.

"I did, for a moment."

"Did he, was he…" Officer Foster couldn't seem to get the words out.

"He didn't seem to be in pain. He didn't remember what happened." The police chief, Ria Franklin, walked over and shook my hand.

"Thanks for coming, Roa. This is a tragedy for the whole department." I didn't mind Franklin, she was better than the last Chief, but I didn't really work with her. "You'll have anything you need to find what did this."

"Thanks, Chief, we'll get them, I promise." I didn't promise often, but for Howard, I would. She gave me a nod and walked out of the room. I sighed, "Hey, can we move the bodies yet?" I turned to the officer in charge of the scene.

"You got gloves?" He yelled across the room. I held up my blue latex covered hands. He nodded. "Go ahead, but be careful."

"Don't have to tell me twice." I kneeled next to Thicket and turned her over in one smooth motion. She hadn't been dead long, but there was no more bleeding. She was stiff, but not so much that I would snap something off. Thank goodness for the little things. There was a large gash in her abdomen, and though I wasn't an expert in elven anatomy, it looked like there might be bits missing. "Do you have a flashlight?" I asked Moss. He quickly took a little mag light off his key chain and shined it in Thicket's wound. *Nice to work with someone who can anticipate my needs.* "Captain!" I waved him over with my bloody glove. I could hear the carpet squishing as he got closer. You never realize how much blood a person has until it's spilled on a carpet you have to walk through.

"Find something?"

"Found a lack of something. Whoever did this took both their hearts." The captain sighed heavily, careful not to wipe his face since he was still wearing gloves.

"So, what, a werewolf or something?" I looked around at the room. Besides the dead bodies of Howard, Thicket, and their pet puca, the room looked to be intact. Usually, a werewolf attack was chaos personified. But here, there were no broken chairs, no claw marks on the walls or on the bodies. The wounds were made with precision. They were too clean, too straight. Claw wounds tend to be more ragged and messier. Now, I could say all this to the officers, who should know these things as well, but my friend just died, and I needed to be a smart-ass.

"Does it look like a full moon outside?" I said sarcastically and pointed to the window. The captain and Moss looked outside. "Uh, yeah."

"What?" I turned and saw a bright full moon through the open window. *Damn it, how could I forget!* "Uh, I mean, it's possible, but with this almost pristine crime scene, I wouldn't peg a werewolf, something sneakier perhaps. Howard doesn't remember what happened. He may never remember since the incident was quite violent." I knelt and pointed at Thicket's empty cavity. "Usually, werewolves aren't so neat with their kills and like to eat body parts, not just hearts, so keep your mind open to other possibilities." I stood and closed my eyes. I put my hands together, palm to palm, and shifted my right hand down and my left hand up. Keeping my palms together, I raised my arms into the air and cast my spell. "Spirits of the other side, show me the crime that has taken my friend from me." I felt my magic spread around the room, and I opened my eyes. It would only show me the last few hours, so hopefully, it hadn't been that long. It didn't take long before I saw the ghosts of the past, well, not the literal ghosts, a memory.

Howard and Thicket were running into the bedroom. He was holding his wife's hand. "All right, they ran into the bedroom, I assume from the dining room, since there was a glass knocked over." Officers around me began writing down what I saw. I watched as the couple stopped by the bed, the puca asleep on the end of it. "They stopped over there by the bed.

Their pet looks like it was asleep on it. It wasn't alerted to anything until they ran in." Something had scared them, but I couldn't see whatever they were staring at. I followed Howard's gaze. Whatever this was, it was big. "Damn it, whatever killed them, cloaked themselves magically," I said. "No one would see it enter or leave, and I can't see it with my spell."

"If it was cloaked, how did they know to run?" Another officer asked.

"I don't know, maybe Thicket could still see it? Elves have a better sense of those things than humans." I watched as their pet puca jumped what seemed like seven feet in the air and sank its little teeth into the attacker. I gasped. "Their pet, bag it and be careful. It bit whatever killed them. I might be able to get something out of it and track the thing."

"It's on its way to the morgue as we speak," Moss said.

"Perfect, thanks." I watched the invisible creature rip through Howard and his wife, telling the officers what happened and how. The thing definitely stole their hearts before leaving. I had seen worse over the years, but not to my friends. I closed my eyes and lowered my arms to end the spell.

"Well, it wasn't a werewolf," I sighed and barely remembered in time not to run my bloody hands through my hair. "I don't know what it was," I raised a finger to the captain as he opened his mouth to complain, but the smart man didn't speak. "Yet."

"Is there anything that uses the moon like a werewolf?" Moss asked.

I shook my head and walked from the room. "No, nothing is so tied to the moon like a werewolf. Some spells do require different moon phases. Since it took their hearts, I assume it plans to do a spell. I'll have to do some research. Moss?" I turned and jumped a little. I didn't hear him walk up behind me.

"Yes, Ms., er Lily."

"Care to escort me back to my car?"

He nodded. "My pleasure." We headed towards the front door, carefully pulling our bloody gloves and booties off.

"I'm going to go to the M.E.'s and check on the puca, care to join me?"

He nodded but scrunched his nose. "Not the cutest pet."

"Probably was to her. They're usually known for luck, but I guess it didn't help tonight." I deposited my little booties and stained gloves in the medical waste bag a rookie was holding. Next crime scene he may get to do something a bit more interesting, like hand out the booties!

Moss and I got into my car, and we headed over to the M.E.'s office downtown. It was in the basement of the police station, which came in handy. "So, Moss, you have a first name?"

"Richard."

"Richard Moss, it sounds like a detective name."

He chuckled. "Does it?"

"To me. How long have you been a detective?"

"A year. I transferred here from Oregon two weeks ago. There weren't any detective jobs available where I was, so I went where there was a need."

"How do you like it here?"

He nodded. "It's nice, smaller than I'm used to, but I like that I can walk to a lot of places."

"Ah, you must live in the Rosewood district. It attracts a lot of newcomers because of the walkability."

"Yeah, it's nice. Are you from Arion?"

"Bred and born." The radio was playing softly, and I realized it was one of Howard's favorite songs. My eyes started to water, but I cleared my throat and blinked them away. "So, Howard gave you my number?" I asked. It probably wasn't the best idea to talk about him, but I needed something to focus on.

"Yeah. He said you were the best of the three witches they had on retainer. How long did you know him?"

"About six years. I gave him a hard time when I first started, but he dished it out, too." I chuckled to keep from crying. "Most other police officers take everything so personally, Howard could joke around. I liked that about him." My lower lip quivered a moment before I bit it into submission. *No crying around the cute detective*, I told myself.

"It's okay to be sad. He was your friend," Moss said.

I sniffed and loudly cleared my throat. "I know. And I will be sad, but later. I have to find his killer first."

He nodded. "Fair enough."

CHAPTER TWO

It took us ten minutes to get to the M.E.'s office. Plenty of time for a speeding ambulance to get there first. I parked in the basement, and we walked into the morgue. It was bright, cold, and smelled like disinfectant.

"Nicola, you here?" I called out. I heard quick footsteps and watched Dr. Nicola Stroud round the corner. She was tall, blonde, and British. She defined herself as a triple threat, and for this town, it was true. I was short, brunette, and local, the exact opposite, but we made a hell of a team at the bars.

"What the bloody hell did those guys bring me?" She was also extremely non-magical and super scientific, so she knew almost nothing about creatures if they weren't human. "It looks like a mutated rat." She crossed her arms over her stomach and tapped her Jimmy Choo covered foot.

I chuckled. "It's a puca. I keep telling you Nicola, you should study something other than humans occasionally. Then these things wouldn't scare you so much."

She scoffed and motioned for us to follow her. "It didn't scare me, it's just weird." We followed her into one of the exam rooms, where the puca was laid out on a metal table. She was right, it wasn't cute, but I'm not fey. It might have been downright adorable to them. Especially when it was alive. "From my meager examination of this puca, it died from blunt force trauma to the body. Whatever hit it was big and strong. X-rays show the ribs, or what I assume are ribs, were broken by something at least six inches wide, causing comminuted fractures and ruptured all the internal organs."

"Meaning?" I put on some gloves and nudged the body with a finger. It felt squishier than I thought it should.

"It means all the ribs this creature had are now in tiny bits, and its guts are goo."

I looked up, impressed and a little scared. "Yikes. My spell showed me it had bit whatever killed Howard and his wife, then got thrown across the room. I guess it was the creature hitting it that broke all its ribs."

Nicola's pretty face turned sad. "Howard? Oh

bollocks." She held up a hand, "Wait, he had a wife?" she asked, leaning back on another exam table.

"A fey wife, as it turns out," Moss said.

Nicola looked behind me like she didn't even notice he was there. "You're Moss, right?" She pointed at him.

"Yeah, Detective Richard Moss." He held out his hand, and she shook it.

"Right, you're the big shot from Oregon, aren't you? Is it as wet as they say it is?" She asked.

"That's Seattle." He said with a smile.

"Oh, you're from Seattle?" Nicola asked. I hid my snicker as best I could. I knew what she was doing.

"No, I'm from Oregon, I just meant," He put his hands up. "Never mind."

Nicola and I smiled at each other before she cleared her throat. "Well, Lily, I'll let you do your witchy thing," Nicola said, wiggling her fingers in the air. "Let me know if you need anything."

"Will do, thanks."

"Bye, Seattle." She waved at Moss as she walked from the room.

"It's...Oregon." He said halfheartedly. "She was teasing, wasn't she?"

"Yep. Quite spectacularly, too." I leaned over the puca's head. Thankfully, it died with its mouth open. I hated prying on dead stuff. I saw two things in the puca's mouth. One was on a back tooth, and the other was down its throat. If I were lucky, one of them would be something from the killer.

My arms broke out in goosebumps, but I ignored it. "Can you hand me one of those long cotton swabs?" I asked, not looking up. One appeared in my line of sight, so I took it without looking up. "Thanks."

"Huh? For what?" I looked up and saw Moss was standing across the room, looking at a model of the human body on the wall.

"The swab." He shrugged like he had no idea what I was talking about. "Never mind." I ducked back to the puca's mouth and ran the cotton swab along the back tooth. It came away with a single hair. Nicola was always organized, so the box of plastic evidence bags was already on the exam table. So I pulled one out and put the entire swab in it.

"What's that?" My ear twitched, and when I turned back to the puca, I saw a bare finger poking the dead pet.

"What the hell are you doing? Don't touch it!"

"I didn't!" I looked up and saw Moss was still across the room. I sighed and turned to my right and saw Will standing next to the table. He was a ghost who haunted the basement and the reason for my sudden goosebumps. He was ornery, but I mostly tolerated him because he was quite handsome for a dead guy.

"E'llo Will," I said in my worst accent. He rolled his eyes. He was Scottish and hated when I made fun of his accent.

"Uck, ya may be able to see the dead, but your accent will always be terrible." He walked around the table and stared at Moss, who had no idea what was going on.

"Who's Will?" he asked as the handsome ghost flipped up the bottom of his jacket, making Moss jump a bit.

I couldn't help but chuckle. "Ignore him, he's just a nuisance."

"Yes, but a rather handsome one, eh?" The ghost winked at me.

"And dead, which rather trumps the handsome bit."

Moss chuckled. "He's handsome?"

I shrugged. "For a dead guy, what do you want Will?"

He walked back over to the exam table. "Just bored. That a puca?"

"Yep. Know anything about them?"

He nodded his head and clicked his tongue. "Some. Elves like to make 'em into pets. It's said they can change their shape, but guess that's a load."

"A load?"

Will shrugged. "A load of shite. If it was tryin'

to defend their master, you'd 'think it'd make itself bigger."

"Hmm, makes sense."

Will shook his head sadly. "Takes something right evil to kill one o' them. Killin' a lucky thing? Must be desperate."

"It killed Howard and his Elven wife," I said.

Will looked up, his jaw dropped. "Not Howie, he was a good un'."

Moss walked over next to me, searching the room for Will. "So, you're talking with a ghost, I take it?"

"Yeah. He haunts the basement, sometimes upstairs." I looked up at Will. He just winked at me.

"What, uh, what does he look like?"

Will lifted his arms and, with a mischievous smile, started turning in a circle. "Yeah love, describe me like one of your Italian girls."

I scoffed and rolled my eyes. "That's not the saying, you limey tit." I looked up a few good Scottish insults when I learned where he was from, but I decided to go with British ones. They annoyed him the most.

Will rolled his eyes. "I'm Scottish woman!" And preceded to bang his head on the metal table next to us. It was loud to me, but I knew to Moss he'd only see the table vibrating slightly.

"He's around twenty-five, I think," I looked

back at Moss, who, to my surprise, seemed to be legitimately curious. Most people get a little nervous when you describe the invisible dead guy in the room. "He says he doesn't remember how old he was, but it could be he didn't even know himself when he was alive."

"I'm sure I had better things to do," Will said, his head laying still on the table.

"Yes, I'm sure you did." I turned back to Moss. "He's just wearing a plain whiteish shirt and dark pants, probably from the eighteen hundreds." Will nodded and stood straight as he flipped an instrument from the wall onto the exam table next to us. Moss jumped at the activity but kept asking questions. I had a feeling he didn't want the dead guy to think he was afraid of him.

"Why is he, um, here?"

I shrugged. "No one's too sure why a ghost haunts. They'll give you any excuse under the sun, but who knows if it's true."

"I see. So, is seeing ghosts a witch thing, or is it just you?" He was so curious it was refreshing.

I turned back to Will. "Why don't you go upstairs and mess with the night crew. There's lots of rookies right now."

He turned to me with a smile and wiggled his eyebrows. "Ooh, fun." He gave me a salute and walked from the room. I leaned against the table facing Moss, careful not to cross my arms, which might contaminate my gloves.

"Any witch can cast a spell to speak with the dead." His eyes widened, and I knew I had to rephrase my wording. "Not like zombie dead, a ghost. But I don't need to. It's an innate talent for me."

Moss looked impressed for a moment. "I don't know if I could get used to seeing ghosts everywhere."

I shrugged. "It takes a while, but it has its uses." Everyone knew about magic, but only a few were blessed with the ability to use it, so some ostracized us, and others were insanely jealous, which would turn them into angry mobs who insisted we were the evil ones. Thankfully, this town was prone to just ignore us.

I picked up another long cotton swab and stuck it down the puca's throat. "One more thing, then I'll try and track whatever did this to Howard." When I pulled the swab out, it had a small piece of cloth on the end.

Moss walked up next to me and looked at what I had. "So, whatever it was, it had clothes on?"

"It had something on. I got a hair from the tooth. If we're lucky, it's from the monster and not a puca hair. It's long for the puca, though." I said, comparing the sample hair to the puca. There was a yell and a clatter of metal items on the floor. Moss put his hand on his sidearm but thankfully didn't pull it. Nicola came rushing in. Her hair was sticking out of the nice bun she had it in earlier.

"Damn it, Will, leave me be! I don't know how you stand him, Lily."

I tried hard to hide my smile. "It's not as fun to mess with me since I can see him. I told him to go bug the rookies."

"Good!" She huffed and straightened her lab coat. "Did you find what you need?"

"I found something, I won't know if it's what I need until I start my spell. Thanks, Nicola."

"No problem." She sighed loudly. I put the evidence bags in my pocket and motioned for Moss to follow me into the parking garage.

"I need to see if any of these things belong to the murderer." He opened the door to the parking garage and held it open for me. "Do you want me to drop you somewhere?"

He stopped and thought for a moment. "Well, my car is here, but if you need help, I can stick around."

I smiled. "All right then. Back to my place."

Before I turned to my car, I could feel power in the air. It was heavy and old. I turned and saw someone leaning against the passenger side door of my car. "Shit," I whispered.

"What?" Moss stepped up next to me.

"An elf." I cleared my throat and made my way over to my car. "Good evening," I stopped a few feet in front of the elf. He was shorter than me, and it was clear he was old. His light blue skin was wrinkled, but he still looked strong. He was dressed in green, but it was hard to tell if it was cloth or leaves. As he bowed, his long, green braid fell over his shoulder.

"You are the witch, Lily Roa?"

"I am. What can I do for you?" He walked closer, his bare feet making no noise on the concrete. I could smell flowers, trees, and wind, although there was none nearby.

"I have heard an elf was murdered this night by the name of Thicket. Is this so?" I didn't normally divulge ongoing investigation information, but I had a feeling if I didn't this time it might get ugly. Elves tended to be peaceful creatures unless something angered them, and it could be hard to predict what might set them off.

I looked back at Moss, and he gave me a nod of approval. "Unfortunately, yes, the elf in question was identified as Thicket. Did you know her?"

He sighed and lowered his head. "I told her living in the human world would lead to her death." His voice was quiet, and I swore I could hear it waver just a bit. "I am her father, Lathai." He held out his hand and I gave it a gentle shake. His skin was warm and soft, and my shoulders relaxed a bit. He was taking the sad route instead of anger. We were lucky.

"I am so sorry for your loss, Lathai. This is Detective Moss. He's helping me in my investigation." Moss stepped around me, shook the elf's hand, and gave a nod. "At the moment, we aren't sure what killed them, but I hope to,"

"Them?" Lathai interrupted.

Moss cleared his throat. "Thicket and her husband, Howard. He was a police officer, so this murder is personal to us."

"Her...husband?" Lathai's head tilted in confusion.

Shit. I leaned closer to Moss. "Howard told me they kept it quiet." *Please don't freak out, please don't freak out.*

Lathai laid his head in his hand. "She married a human. No wonder such a fate befell her."

"Well, I don't think," Moss started, but I stomped back on his foot to get him to shut up. Thankfully, he did.

The grieving father looked up, his ancient eyes teary. "When you find her murderer, you will contact me." He handed me an acorn which seemed to appear from nothing, and with a wave of his arm a portal appeared, and he walked through. We watched it close behind him, and I leaned against my car with a big sigh. "That could have been worse. Sorry about your foot."

He snickered. "It's fine. Are elves dangerous? I assumed they were mostly peaceful."

"They can be dangerous with the right incentive. He certainly has incentive now." I looked at the acorn in the palm of my hand. It seemed mundane. I couldn't even sense a hint of magic on it, but I knew to the mourning father, it meant more. I tucked it in my pocket and unlocked my car. "Shall we?"

CHAPTER THREE

We walked into my apartment around midnight. I could still smell the pizza I ordered earlier and felt my stomach growl.

"Down girl, we have to work."

Moss took off his jacket and looked around. "You have a pet?"

"Pet? Oh, I was talking to my stomach," I said while giving it a pat.

He chuckled. "I thought I smelled pizza. Lovely place." I loved my apartment. The building only had six other units, and mine was the biggest up in the attic. The exposed brick gave it a homey feel, and the dark wood in the kitchen made it my favorite room in the apartment.

"Thanks. It pays being one of only three people in town who willingly talk to the dead." He sat on my dark red couch, and I could tell he was nervous as his eyes darted around the place. I would be, too, if it was the first time I saw a witch in action. "You okay?" I asked, partially teasing.

"I just don't want to get in the way."

"You won't." I walked to the room just off the living room. Fancy people might call it a parlor, but I dubbed it my 'witchy' room. I kept all my supplies in there. Candles, herbs, oils, and books upon books. Whatever I needed was in here. I loved how it smelled, patchouli and sea salt. It was an odd combination to some, but it made me happy. I picked up a clear glass bowl, three red tea candles, and some rose oil. I put them on the living room table and pulled a chair close. As much as I loved my witchy room, it wasn't always the best place to cast spells. Especially since this spell required fire, and currently, I had dried herbs hanging from the ceiling in there. "Moss, can you fill this bowl with some water for me?" He quickly got to his feet and did as I asked. It was cute. I put some rose oil in my right hand and rubbed it on each tea candle. Moss set the bowl on the table in front of me without spilling a drop. "Thank you, Igor."

He snickered and sat on the couch across from me. "So, what are you doing?"

"I'm going to see if I can get a picture of our killer." I put the candles in the water and lit them with the snap of my fingers.

"Whoa." I looked up and saw Moss staring at the three little fires.

"You're just adorable, aren't you?" I teased.

He smiled. "If the lady who can summon fire with a snap of her fingers says I'm adorable, I'm adorable." I laughed. I didn't normally do magic in front of people who weren't used to it, but maybe he would get used to it? Howard did, after all. First, I took the black cloth from the puca's throat and dipped it in the rose oil.

"Let's start with this. I don't relish the smell of burning hair, no matter how small a quantity." I cleared my throat and took a calming breath. "Spirits, find for me the one who killed my friend," I dipped the cloth in the water. "Find for me the one who killed his wife," I glanced up at Moss for a second, police officers can get kind of pissy about destroying evidence, but he seemed to understand. His eyes met mine, and all I saw was curiosity and the fire. His eyes were green, but I could see little flecks of brown in them. I cleared my throat and shook my head. Damn fire, trying to make things romantic during a murder investigation. I lowered the cloth close to the middle flame as the other two flames curled in to meet, creating one big flame. "Tell me who stole these people from our lives." The cloth burned into nothing, and smoke curled up from the candles. I sat back and watched the smoke turn into a creature. But it was becoming increasingly corporeal, which wasn't supposed to happen. "No."

"I take it that's not supposed to happen?" Moss got to his feet and moved behind the couch.

"No, it's not." I stood, and the smoke stretched and curled into a bigger shape. "It's just supposed to make a small shape above the water. I don't know what this is." I walked around the chair, Moss pulled his gun, but I motioned for him to put it away. "That won't do any good here," I said calmly. The smoke stretched from the table to the ceiling and growled as it turned to me.

"You can't stop us, little witch," It growled, sounding like several voices speaking at the same time. "We have the hearts. It's only a matter of time before we're free." A hideous face formed in the smoke, leathery with yellow eyes, and it quickly flew through me and dissipated.

"Lily!" Moss ran around the couch and grabbed onto my arms. "Are you okay?" I was cold, but it was just a memory of what had killed Howard and his wife. It couldn't hurt me.

"Yeah," I laid my hands on my chest, "yeah, I'm fine." I took a breath and looked up at him. "I know what killed them." I reached into my pocket and pulled out the hair I had pulled from the puca, and handed it to him, I wouldn't be needing it now.

His eyes went wide. "You do? What was it?" He put the bag with the hair in his pocket.

I sighed and sank into the chair. "Sluagh."

"Slew-ha?" He said slowly, "What's that?"

"Sluagh, it's an Irish spirit. Composed of several evil spirits that have been rejected by the afterlife. They're nasty."

"It said something to you, didn't it? I heard it growling, but it sounded like it might be talking." He pulled out a little notebook and pen.

I snapped my fingers, and the tea candles went out. "It said it had the hearts and that it was only a matter of time before they were free."

"I take it that's bad?" He asked as he wrote down what I said.

I sat back and sighed. "If it means all the evil spirits making it up would be individually free, yeah, that's bad."

"How many of them are there?"

"Anywhere from three to ten, depends really." I got up and ran into my witchy room and started searching for a helpful book. By the tenth unhelpful one, I was getting frustrated. I held out my hands, "*Libra cor meum!*" Two books flew from the shelves, and one landed in my hands. But I missed the other one, and it hit Moss in the back.

"Ow!" He jumped to the side and rubbed his

back.

"Sorry, didn't realize you were in here." I picked up the book and rubbed his back before I plopped onto the couch. I opened it up and wiggled my fingers over the pages. They flipped back and forth until the page I wanted showed up. "Okay, here's something." I scooted over so Moss could sit, but when I looked up, I saw he was still standing in the other room. "You okay? That book didn't sever your spine, did it?"

He stared at me for a few moments, then smiled. "No, I'll live, you were saying?" He sat on the couch and looked at the book.

"This spell here uses the hearts of lovers to give you your heart's desire. If this creature's desire is to no longer be Sluagh, to be free, this could be the spell he's using."

"That's…horrific." Moss shook his head as he wrote that information in his notebook.

"When murder is involved, it usually is." I kept reading. The spell was to take place on holy ground, which meant either a church or a cemetery. It also said a full moon at its apex was required. "Uh-oh."

"What?" Moss leaned over and looked at the book again.

"It says the spell requires a full moon." I looked over at him, "It's going to," Moss's face was close. Those brown specks in his eyes were getting bigger.

"Um, we need to get to the nearest church or cemetery to the murder scene. The moon will reach its apex in about an hour. We need to find it before then."

He nodded. "You want to split up?"

"No! Um, I uh, I just mean, it could use either of those places. *We* don't have to split up. In fact, I think it's a bad idea if we do."

"Right." He pulled out his cell and stood up as he called someone. I sat back and took a breath. It had been a while since I was so close to a good-looking guy who wasn't dead. "Hey, sergeant, it's Moss. We got a lead on Howard's killer. Yes. Ms. Roa said it was a Slew-ha?" I watched him shrug as he spoke. "I don't know, but I have a feeling we'll know it when we see it. We need to search churches and cemeteries close to the crime scene. According to Ms. Roa, we have about an hour before this creature is let loose on the city, so to speak." He paced a bit while the sergeant spoke. "Okay, we'll take the cemetery, I'll call if we find anything. If you see it, let us know, and we'll meet you there." He hung up and held his hand out to me. "We're going to Rosemont Cemetery, and the sarge will take a group to St. Michael's." I took his hand, and he helped me to my feet. "It's a few blocks away from the cemetery."

"Right, I know where it is." I felt him give my hand a squeeze before I walked back into my witchy room. If I was going to stop a Sluagh, I needed some tricks up my sleeve.

CHAPTER FOUR

I pulled into Rosemont Cemetery and parked by the offices. "So, will we be able to tell if it's here?" Moss asked as he switched the clip on his gun from regular bullets to silver ones. I wasn't sure they would work any better, but it couldn't hurt to try.

"Oh yeah, we will." I pulled the parking brake on my car, and we both closed our doors as quietly as we could. I could feel heavy, dark magic emanating from the far end of the cemetery. My skin began to crawl, and my fingertips were tingly. Dark magic always messes with you. Mundane people would assume there's something wrong inside their bodies to make them feel cold and tingly for no reason, but it's almost always magic. If it bothered Moss, he didn't show it. "It's definitely here." Moss took out his cell phone and texted the sergeant about the creature being in the cemetery.

"They'll be here soon." I nodded and led the way inside. Rosemont was the second oldest of the five cemeteries in town. No one had been buried here in at least a hundred years. There were more mausoleums than graves, and they were lavishly decorated for buildings that housed dead people. My favorite was the one belonging to the Marcher family. It had a huge angel on top, made of black marble with gold veins running through it. I wondered if Moss would like it. I shook the thought of such a weird date from my mind and concentrated on the magic I felt. The closer we got, the darker the magic felt. It made me shiver, and my heart sped up. We weren't supposed to be around this, and it let me know. It was an effective way to keep mundane people away. All they'd feel was a sense of unease, which would make them leave. But we couldn't leave. We had to find this creature. We walked through the headstones. The grass was already misty and muted our footsteps. I pulled out my little hex bag, filled with feathers, sage oil, some tacks, and a piece of charcoal. Hopefully, all together with the spell, the hearts will be made useless, and Howard and his wife will be at peace. I stopped next to a broken-down mausoleum and pulled out my pocket knife.

"What are you doing?" Moss asked as he flattened against the wall.

I pricked my finger and squeezed. "I need to

mark the bag before I throw it." I drew a smiley face with my blood, and I saw Moss looking skeptical. "It doesn't matter what it looks like. The blood shows possession. The spell I found requires the caster to put the hearts in fire, so I'm counting on there being one. I'll throw the bag in the fire, and when I give the word, the spell will go off. I'm hoping that will make the hearts useless."

He nodded. "If you say so." He pulled his sidearm and made sure the safety was on. "I know it might not do much, but I'd feel a little better with it out."

"I just drew a smiley face in blood on a magic bag. I'm not going to look at you funny for having your sidearm out." He smiled, and we slowly moved around the crumbling mausoleum. A few yards later, I saw a fire through some bushes. *Yes.* I stopped and pointed it out to Moss, who nodded and started for a flanking position. I assumed, at least, because up until this point, he followed me around like a puppy. A cute puppy with green eyes who didn't seem to mind the magic.

I headed towards the fire and held the hex bag in my right hand. I moved around the several feet of bushes and got a clear view of the area. Next to the fire, laying on some flat stones, were two hearts. I didn't see the Sluagh, so I quickly tossed the hex bag into the fire.

"*Du'flet*," I whispered and watched the hearts wither instantly. The smoke of the fire curled into two distinct shapes, one human, the other elven. "Howard," I whispered and smiled as I watched him embrace his elven love. It was easy to see the two loved each other a great deal in life as their shapes pressed close and became one. I watched the smoke float away towards the stars. They were finally at peace. "Bye, Howard." I looked across the way at Moss. He was staring at the smoke as well. You didn't need magic eyes to see the freed lovers. From the small smile on his face, I could tell he was moved at the sight.

"Wow," he mouthed and looked over at me. *Wow, indeed, Detective.* A screech filled the air, and I was ripped from the happy scene back to reality and covered in goosebumps to boot. My brain told me to run and get away, but the noise was made to scare me. It wouldn't hurt me. I took a few breaths and saw Moss running at me.

"What the hell is that?" he whisper-yelled and stopped next to me.

"It's trying to scare us."

"Well, it's working." We turned back to the fire, and I saw a huge black mass erupt from the nearby trees. It looked like it was running straight for us. I held up my hand, ready for a spell, but as it got next to the fire, it stopped. It formed a more solid shape of a cloaked body, and I saw its head look down at the withered hearts.

"We heard a witch was on our tail." Its multiple voices were deep and wispy. Some seemed to echo what others had said. It was disorienting. "You think destroying these hearts will stop us?" It whipped its head up at us. The same deformed face I saw in my apartment made me want to run, but I held my ground. "There are many hearts for us to take. Full moons are once a month. You cannot stop us. The Order brought us forth, and we will do their bidding!" It shot out a shadowy arm, and it wrapped around my neck. "Maybe your heart will do!" It screeched as I felt it force me to my knees. I wasn't choking. It was more to keep me from moving..

"Let her go!" Moss yelled and pointed his gun at it.

Its head turned to him and tilted to the side. "You are protective of her. Perhaps both your hearts will do!" Another shadowy arm shot out and wrapped around his neck. He fired several shots as it forced him to his knees, but it did nothing.

I clapped my hands together and pointed my palms at the fire. "Try this!" I yelled and swiped left like a bad tinder match and flung the fire at it.

The Sluagh screeched as it caught fire but didn't let us go. "No!" Another shadow sprung from its body and tried to put the fire out, but it didn't work. "We have to hurry!" The shadow around my throat sprouted another limb. It was smaller and looked sharp. I gasped as it pierced my skin. The pain was shocking as it made a long cut down my sternum. I could almost hear it scraping against the bone. It was sickening. I had to do something. But the pain was taking my concentration, so I couldn't cast any spells. I looked over at Moss, he had his own sharp shadow to deal with, and the shock on his face as the shadow sliced his chest woke something in me. How dare this thing do this to him! To us! I reached into my pocket, looking for something, anything that could help, when my hand wrapped around the acorn Lathai had given me and threw it on the ground as hard as I could.

It broke, and a moment later, I saw a familiar portal, and the old elf appeared. His face was angry. "You killed my daughter!" He yelled, and the Sluagh let us go. "You will be erased, Sluagh!" Lathai yelled, and I watched the old elf throw something powdery on the shadow creature, who howled as it enveloped him. I jumped as Moss touched my arm. He had crawled over to me while still bleeding on the ground.

"Are you okay?" He pulled out a handkerchief, and even though my cut was nestled neatly between my breasts, he pressed the handkerchief on the cut, trying to stem the flow of blood.

"I'm fine, you?" Not fearing man boobs, I moved his torn shirt aside and saw his wound was still bleeding, but thankfully nothing else was coming out. I didn't have anything else on me, so I pressed my hand against his cut, pressing just as hard as he was on me. The first cut was just for the skin it seemed. I imagine a moment later, it would have pieced our breast bones. I hissed at the stinging pain in my chest and looked up as Lathai created another portal, and the Sluagh was sucked away into the darkness beyond. It closed, and the only sound left was the happy, crackling fire.

Lathai walked over to us and kneeled. "Hold still." He laid his hands on our chests, and I instantly felt the pain melt away. We moved our hands and saw our cuts were completely healed.

"Thank you," I said, then turned to Moss. The only sign of damage was the blood on our torn shirts. I laid my bloody hand on his chest and sighed in relief. I could feel his heart pounding under my fingers. He put his hand over mine and nodded that he was all right.

"You found my daughter's killer. I owed you." Lathai said.

"What happened to the Slew-ah thing?" Moss asked.

"I banished it back to the dark realm where they reside in pain and loneliness forever. I am not sure how it got out. But I will make sure it does not happen again." He waved his hand and stepped through another portal, leaving us alone. Moss stared at the spot, almost frozen with amazement.

"Are you okay?" I asked. It was an awful lot for a non-magical person to take in one day.

He nodded. "I am." He turned back to me and gave my hand a squeeze. "I'm okay. We're alive, and the murderer is being punished. At least, I think it is."

I smiled and took my hand back. "Yes, it is." The sound of sirens and the familiar red and blue lights started lighting up the cemetery around us. "Oh, thank goodness we're saved," I said sarcastically.

Moss laughed and got to his feet. "Thought they'd get here sooner. They must have gotten lost in the cemetery." He held his hand out for me. I took it and stood up.

"This is going to be one interesting report to write, Moss."

He snickered. "Care to help me with it? I don't think I can spell Sluagh."

I smiled. "Probably not, but at least you said it right this time." We waited for the cops to find us so they could start going over the crime scene. Hopefully, they wouldn't get too grouchy about me destroying even *more* evidence, but hey, it had to be done. Moss could vouch for me, besides, I don't know how much evidence a Sluagh would have left anyway if it had been successful in its plans.

***

About an hour later, Moss walked up beside me as I stood against a nearby mausoleum. Our hands were clean thanks to some wet wipes an EMT had given us, and they gave us both a clean bill of health, so there was no need to visit the ER.

"So Detective, with Howard gone, I'm going to need a new —"

"Yes." He answered before I could even finish and gave me a little smile. "I'd love to work with you."

"All this," I motioned to the crime scene where the withered hearts still sat by the fire, "doesn't scare you away?"

He shook his head, his eyes burning into mine. "No."

I smiled. "Good."

When the cops were done questioning us and going over the crime scene, the sun was rising. "Well, Moss, all the bars are closed," I said as we walked to my car. "What do you say we go find some pancakes and toast to Howard?"

"Sounds good. And you can call me Richard."

I smiled and got into my car. "As you wish, Officer Hotty," I said quietly as he climbed in.

"What's that?" he asked as he buckled his

seatbelt.

"Nothing." I smiled and drove towards the nearest breakfast place. We deserved a lot of syrup after last night.

CHAPTER FIVE

A few days later, Howard and his wife Thicket were laid to rest. The entire Albion Police Department was in attendance. He had been a cop for over thirty years, so it was standing room only. A few of his regular arrestees even showed up at the edge of the group to pay their respects. The sun was shining as a sea of black and blue stood around the two graves, themselves covered in flowers. I knew Thicket's casket was empty. Her father had taken her body back the day after the Sluagh was killed. Nobody but me, Nicola, and the funeral director knew. An empty casket would do just fine for everyone else.

Nicola stood next to me, an arm through mine, as we listened to the Pastor talk about Howard's life and all he had accomplished. The funeral was quite spectacular. People stood by the Pastor and told stories about how Howard had influenced their lives. I kept my stories to myself. I had a feeling no one really wanted to hear them.

When people started filing away, I noticed Detective Moss walking towards us and felt Nicola give me a little nudge.

I tried to hide my smile. "I see him," I whispered, hoping no one would hear.

"Ms. Roa, Dr. Stroud, how are you?" He was in his dress blues, he made the uniform look even better.

"Hey, Seattle," Nicola said, and he scoffed with a smile. I told him he could call me Lily, but we were around other cops, so formality was better.

"Detective, could be better." I had done my crying after our celebratory pancake breakfast. I went home, cried my eyes out, then called Jackson and Amelia, the other witches in town, and told them what happened. They were on their way back from Cancun, so at least I didn't ruin their vacation.

"I have something for you." He reached into his uniform jacket and pulled out a picture. "I found it on Howard's desk." I took the picture and smiled. It was of me and Howard after we had captured a rogue magician six years ago. It wasn't the first assignment we did together, but it proved to the department that Howard and I made a good team.

"That was a good day."

"I gotta get back to the morgue." Nicola gave

me a hug. "I'll see you later."

"All right."

Nicola walked away but turned back to us, "You should tell Detective Seattle about that day," she called out and turned with a smile.

"She's going to call me Seattle forever, isn't she?" he asked with a smile.

I nodded. "Probably. Could be worse. You could be Detective Polka Dots."

"Ooh," he laughed, "I'll take Seattle." He looked at his shoes for a moment before meeting my eyes. "Some of us are going to The Wall and have some lunch. Would you like to go?" Butterflies in my stomach made their appearance, but I had to play it calm.

"I would, but I don't really get along with most of the cops. They think I'm weird."

He waved a hand. "Don't worry about them, you'll be with me."

I tucked the picture into my jacket pocket. "Are you sure you want to throw your hat into my ring that fast? Working together is one thing, but being seen in public together is another."

"I know a good cop when I see one. You may not have the badge, but you got everything else. We can make them see it."

I nodded. "You are quite the positive person,

Detective."

***

I met him outside The Wall. It was the fanciest restaurant in Albion. I think what made it fancy was the fact that it had carpet and wood-paneled walls. The food wasn't anything to praise, and the owner didn't like me, so it had been years since I graced them with my presence. Moss held the door open for me, and we walked in. Thankfully, it wasn't like in the movies where you walk in, and everything gets quiet, and people stare. Everyone was too hungry to care. Grieving can make you hungry, for sure.

The server set us at a table by the rest of the department. We got a few looks, but at least we were by ourselves at a table for two. I heard whispering, but I tried to ignore it.

"Thanks for the invite, didn't realize how hungry I was." I sipped the water our server gave us, and we ordered.

"No problem. You were integral in solving Howard's murder, and in less than twenty-four hours, you deserve some free food." I smiled. It was nice being appreciated. "That's a pretty necklace. Where'd you get it?" He pointed at the crystal around my neck.

"Oh, I got this a long time ago." It was a smokey quartz about an inch long, surrounded by wire to keep it on the leather strap around my neck. It wasn't the fanciest looking necklace, but it helped me focus my powers sometimes and acted as an alert system for my apartment, so I wore it everywhere. I was lucky that damn Sluagh didn't cut it when it tried to take my heart. "It's kind of a magical alarm system and can help me if I need to focus." I held it up and I could tell he could see the dark mist swirling around in the crystal.

"Impressive. So, what is your solve rate?"

I smiled. "Hundred percent, you?"

His eyes went wide. "Wow, I don't think the witches at my last department had one hundred."

I shrugged. "Well, it's a small town, it might help."

"I'm about eighty. At least I was in Oregon."

"Hey, Moss!" We turned and saw Jordan, one of the motorcycle cops, motioning at him. "Sure, you wanna sit with her? She might put a love potion in your tea." The officers around him laughed.

"Aww, do you need a love potion Jordan?" I asked, "Maybe a special little blue potion? I bet your wife will thank me." I gave him a wink. Everyone laughed louder and slapped Jordan on the back, who didn't really appreciate the joke. "Why's it always love potions?" I turned back to Moss, "It's like people think love is something to be afraid of."

"It's probably the vulnerability factor," Moss said, "not being in control."

"Yeah, I guess." The server brought our food, I got chicken tenders (a girl needs comfort food after a funeral), and he got a giant bacon burger. Everything smelled good. My chicken was tender and juicy, but the gravy was a bit too peppery for me. Thankfully, there was some honey mustard. Overall, it wasn't bad. Maybe they got a new chef? Moss managed to eat without getting a crumb on his suit. It was impressive. My napkin, however, looked like a toddler tried to do art with food. I don't know how I get so messy eating in public. I try not to!

"So, tell me about the picture," he said, eating a crinkle fry.

"Giving into peer pressure?" I teased.

Moss chuckled. "You know she's going to ask if you told me."

"That's true." I wiped my fingers on my napkin. "It wasn't the first case we worked, but the result showed everyone that Howard was right, and they needed a witch on retainer at the very least. Before me, they just stumbled around the paranormal world. I never understood that."

His eyes went wide at that. "They never had a witch working with the cops before?"

I shook my head. "Nope, small-town mentality, I guess. Anyway, about a month before the picture was taken, several stores in town reported being robbed, but their cameras never caught anything. Clothes, appliances, food even."

"Sounds like someone moved into town."

"Right? So, after weeks of nothing, Howard got ahold of me. He asked if there might be some magic thing I could do to figure out where this stuff went or who took it all. It didn't take long for me to find the trail. We followed it to an abandoned motel outside of town, and low and behold, there was a man living there no one in town knew, and everything in those rooms had been stolen over the past few months. He was using magic to freeze the cameras, and then he'd slip inside using a tunnel spell. He seemed so shocked about being caught, like it had been a long time, if ever, since he had been. I don't particularly remember him having a long rap sheet or anything, but we sent him to prison in the big city because of how much he had stolen, almost twenty thousand dollars' worth of stuff. No idea where he is now."

"So, they probably wouldn't have caught the guy if it weren't for magic." Moss looked impressed, and I tried not to let my cheeks turn red.

"Nope. It's not a flashy story, no hex bags or dead…" I stopped, thinking suddenly of Howard. "A pretty clean case, really."

"Sounds like it. Well, I know I'm new here, but whatever I can do to keep you around, I'll do it. You're clearly an asset."

"Thank you. I appreciate it."

CHAPTER SIX

A week later, I got a text from Moss, but it wasn't a funny meme that he'd been sending lately. There was something weird in the morgue, and he could use my help. Of course, he texted me right then while I was at Intermezzo's, my favorite Italian Restaurant, looking hot in my new red dress about to eat the most perfect bruschetta ever. Perfectly crispy crostini and fresh tomatoes that burst in your mouth and basil that brought all the flavors together, there was nothing like it. I wondered why he texted me about it. There were, after all, two other witches on retainer for the department, Jackson and Amelia Fell. But I assumed they were, once again, unavailable. Or Moss liked me. Truth be told, I wouldn't mind if it were the latter. But getting called by the cops put more money in my pocket, so I looked at the text, thankful he didn't call. It's harder than you'd expect to explain to the family who overheard your conversation that the guy on the other line didn't mean an actual brain-eating zombie. It was a cop code, and I didn't have time to explain sorry, I made your kid cry!

I mean, it technically wasn't a brain-eating zombie. It was an undead cat, so no chance of the zombie apocalypse. But the way the rookie on the other end of the line was acting, it surely was about to be the end of the world! So, lesson learned, don't answer cop calls on speakerphone, or let anyone but my handler call me. But clearly, treating myself was a hint to the universe to interrupt me. At least the restaurant could give me my bruschetta to go.

***

Half an hour later, I was standing next to an exam table in the morgue. Moss stood across from me, his hands on his hips.

"Officers Dax and More found this glorious glob about an hour ago in an alley."

We were both clueless as we stared at a mysterious, almost bowling ball sized glob of green goo that had been plopped on the shiny table between us. I stretched my arms in the air while blowing the loudest raspberry I could.

"PHBBBT!" Moss grimaced as he looked up at me, a mixture of amusement and confusion on his face. "What was that some sort of ancient witch spell?" he teased.

"Yes! Our most powerful spells start with a *phbt*!" I sighed, and my arms slapped against my sides. "I'm thinking! What do you do when you're stumped?"

"I don't stick my tongue out and spit everywhere," he said, trying not to smile. I wrinkled my nose at him. "Snob." He snickered and shook his head as I looked back at the blob, trying to hide my smile from him.

We had been looking at it for about ten minutes and were still no closer to an answer. I knew Moss was as confused as I was. If this was my first giant glob of green goo, I imagine it would be his as well. "So, the officers who found it say it already had these slashes in it?" I pointed to the four deep gashes in what we assumed was the top.

Moss nodded. "Yeah. They weren't sure how they got there. But there weren't any other bits scattered around the alley. I radioed the police officers on patrol to keep an eye out for more little green blobs."

"I bet that was fun for the scanner jockeys to hear." I leaned closer to the blob. I could see my warped reflection in it. I didn't look half bad as a flattened-out pancake.

Richard huffed. "It's not the weirdest call I've had since moving here."

"Oh, just wait. The longer you're here, the

weirder it gets." Moss was a touch over six feet with the broad shoulders of a person who worked out. It was hard to tell if his hair was dark blonde or light brown, but I had fun staring at him, trying to figure it out. You know when there wasn't a crime to solve. Since he was a detective, he wore suits to work instead of a uniform, and I swear he made those suits look better. Anyway, back to the blob.

I slapped on a pair of latex gloves, picked up a piece of litmus paper with tweezers, and laid it on the gelatinous glob. Nothing. "Well, it's not acidic or... soapy, I guess." I poked it with my gloved finger, and it felt like it looked. A big, jiggly blob of jelly.

"Alkalinic?" Moss suggested.

I clapped my gloved hands together and pointed at him. "Yes! That's the word."

He sighed and scratched the back of his neck. "We need to figure out if it's dangerous to the community."

"Well, even though it's my first mysterious green blob," I poked it again, "my professional opinion is it doesn't seem dangerous. It's not moving, it's not acidic, it doesn't even smell. I think the mystery is where it came from."

Nicola came walking around the corner. Her expensive heels clacked on the cheap, laminate floor. Nicola and I were opposites, she was tall, blonde, and that British accent was killer. I was vertically challenged, dark-haired, and had no accent whatsoever, but I've never had a better friend.

"You're awful dressed up for a case," Nicola said with an appreciative smile. "I like what you've done with your hair." I hadn't bothered going back to my apartment to change when Moss called. So, I was still wearing my little red dress, and my dark hair was in one of those fancy twisty braids. At least, I thought it was fancy.

"Thanks. I had a date at Intermezzo's with their bruschetta." I motioned at the takeout box on a nearby counter.

"Ooh, they do use the perfect amount of garlic." She sighed and put her hands on her hips. I had a feeling she wouldn't be enthused with the odd glob on her exam table. She didn't know much about the preternatural. Humans were her bag, according to her. She had petitioned the city to hire a medical examiner who was a preternatural expert, but they told her it was too expensive. So, she got everything from people to werewolves. "So, how disgusting is it this time?"

I smiled as big as I could and pointed at the green blob with the double gun gesture. I figured it would make it more exciting, but she just gave her usual groan and put her perfectly manicured hands into her gloves.

"Gorgeous, isn't it?" I teased.

"You and I have different definitions of the word gorgeous. But it's fascinating. I'll give you that." Her eyes scanned the blob. "No reaction to the litmus?"

I shook my head. "Nothing."

"And we're sure it's not Jell-O?"

"Pretty sure, it doesn't smell like anything and doesn't fall apart or melt like Jell-O."

"It's surprisingly sturdy," Moss added.

"Well," she sighed and stood straight. "I specialize in bodies, not goo."

"There's goo in bodies." I pointed out, but she wasn't taking the bait as she shook her head 'no' at me. "This could be a body!" I suggested motioning to the table. "You know, a different kind of body."

Nicola's pretty face scrunched up like she just smelled roadkill. "We don't even know if it's alive! What if I start cutting through it, and it starts screaming?"

"Stop cutting," Moss suggested. I couldn't stop the snicker that escaped, and Nicola gave him the evil eye.

"Yes, thank you, Detective." she sighed and crossed her arms. "Okay, I'll try and remove a piece and run a few tests. You're leaving it here, I assume?"

"Yeah. I just got a new couch. I'm not taking it home. What if it starts moving around?"

Nicola rolled her eyes. "Uck, thanks for the visual. Hand me a scalpel, would you?" I turned and picked up the sharp instrument and handed it, handle first, to Nicola. She took it and, with one more shake of her head, cut into the gelatinous blob. We all waited a moment for a scream, but nothing happened. I swear we all breathed out in relief at the same time. I don't think any of us wanted to hear a gelatinous orb scream or gurgle in pain. She got a sizeable chunk off the side and started dividing it into more pieces. "I'll let you know if I find anything, but don't hold your breath."

"Got it, have fun!" I slipped my plastic gloves off and tossed them in the biohazard bin.

"We still on for Saturday?" she asked, nose deep in green goo.

"Yep, unless a certain Detective needs my beautiful brain for anything," I said, looking at Moss.

"I'll try not to ruin your night out." He smirked as we walked upstairs into the bullpen. The medical examiners were in the basement of the precinct, which was convenient. It was one big happy, murder-solving family. We opened the door to the bullpen, and even though it was nine at night, the noise went from quiet to cacophonous in one easy push. The large room was all dark wood and metals, a total dude cave. Moss's desk was off to the right by the large, frosted windows. We walked over, and he sat at his desk, and I took the chair next to it. His desk was always a little messy. Crushed paper cups and files all over the place, but I don't judge. I tend to think the smarter ones are always a little messy. And that's not in any way an excuse for my own messes. "Well, at least no one died on this one," he said.

"That we know of."

"Ooh," he chuckled, "unsettling."

I shrugged. "I'm probably a bit jaded. You'll have to excuse me."

"Hey, it's a way to stay sane." He wrote something on a notepad, "You and Nicola go out a lot?"

I shrugged. "We try to go out a few times a month. But you know, crime waits for no woman. No matter how much she needs to dance to techno music while taking multi-colored shots out of a long test tube."

"Ha! Sounds like quite the night," he said, shuffling through the files on his desk.

"You have no idea. You have to go two towns over for that kind of fun." The left side of his mouth tilted in a smile, and I noticed a little dimple on his cheek.

"Hey, Bruja!" A yell tore me from staring at the newly discovered dimple, and I turned. Mickey Torrico, a down on his luck construction worker, was being led into a holding cell. There was a four-day beard on his face, and he looked like he was sweating tequila. "I'm innocent this time! Tell them!" he yelled at me.

I scoffed and rolled my eyes. "Of what?"

"I was drinking beer! I don't get drunk on beer!" The bullpen erupted in laughter. "I don't!" They dragged Mickey through a doorway, and he disappeared.

"What'd he call you?" Moss asked.

I looked over at him. He seemed genuinely curious. "Bruja. It's Spanish for Witch."

"I see." Moss was still new to our little haven of Arion. He came from Oregon, so I don't think he really understood the small-town mentality. He'll find out soon just how well I was known. Especially when it got out that he was working with me. "Why does Mickey think you could tell them he was innocent?"

I shrugged. "Well, I'm a witch, so of course I can tell if he's drunk off his ass or not."

"Ah, because witches are omnipotent when it comes to drunks." He teased.

I couldn't stop the chuckle from my lips. "He's one of the few in town who were friends with my family before they died. He never believed the rumors about me either, so I tolerate him."

Richard's eyes softened. "I didn't know your

family died."

I shrugged. "It was a long time ago."

"Well, I'm sorry anyway." Richard leaned back in his chair, putting his hands on the back of his head. "The other witches, Amelia and Jackson Fell are they married or brother and sister? I haven't met them yet."

That's because you always call me. "They're married. They moved to town a few years ago, but they like to keep a low profile." Being a witch in a small town was like walking on a thin wire with razor shoes. You never knew when it was going to snap and turn you into a pariah. I was four when the wire snapped for me, so I was used to it. They moved from a big city, so they weren't. You'd think growing up in a world with magic would make people more tolerant, but there are always those who want to push a mundane agenda. Let's blame magic for all the bad stuff in the world! You get used to it. I wish we didn't have to. "You got any plans this weekend?" I asked, trying not to seem like I was fishing for a date.

Moss cleared his throat and shook his head. "No, still trying to organize my office at home. Might try and finally get it done."

"Sounds fun." The sarcasm was heavy.

He smiled. "It will be when it's done. I can finally—" A scream filled the air, and every police officer in the room got to their feet.

"Was that Mickey?" I asked. Major Ryan rushed out of the holding area. He looked irritated as he stalked over to me. I assumed I was the cause of his irritation since his eyes were burning into mine. He hated me and the other witches. He thought we were a waste of money even though our solve rate was one hundred percent. I snuck a glance at Moss, who gave me a sympathetic look. No one likes it when the major is on a war path.

"Roa, go get rid of that asshole," he demanded as he stopped in front of me. I got to my feet and looked up at him. Ryan was tall, but most were compared to me. His moustache was twitching, and I fought not to giggle.

"I assume you aren't talking about Mickey, Major?" I mean, he was being vague, I swear I wasn't trying to bait the guy!

"No, I don't mean Mickey, Roa!" he roared. "That damn ghost! He's screwing with Mickey, and it's freaking his drunk ass out. I don't need a freaked out drunk in my hold! What kind of witch are you if you can't get rid of a ghost!" He turned and went back to his office without an answer. I rolled my eyes and walked across the bullpen to the holding area. I could feel everyone's eyes on me. They all knew how the major felt about witches, and even though most didn't like me, they knew how important we were to the department. But that didn't mean they'd come to my rescue when Ryan was mad. So, I pretended everyone was looking at me because I looked smoking hot in my little red dress. Which I did.

I turned the corner and saw Mickey sitting on a bench in the holding cell. His eyes were wide as they darted around the enclosure.

"Oh! Bruja, help me! The spirits are punishing me. Get rid of them!" Will was in the cell with him, laughing and rolling on the floor. I had no idea it was so funny messing with the living. Then again, Mickey was incredibly drunk and even the living couldn't resist that. Don't tell me you've never been to a party where a passed-out drunk person got a dick drawn on their face. I walked to the cell and stared at Will for a moment.

When he finally realized I was there, he got to his feet. "Ahh, Lily, look at 'cha. You look nice! Got a hot date? If not, want one?" His eyebrows wiggled suggestively. The Scottish ghost was good looking for a dead guy. It was the one reason I put up with him. It could also be the reason I hadn't exorcised him from the precinct. He seemed happy enough haunting the old building. Will wore an old-fashioned shirt that might have been white once but was covered in stains and dark pants. Typical peasant wear, according to Nicola. When he turned around, I could see the wound in his head made from a hammer most like. He didn't seem to be aware of it, but I never asked about it either. The last thing anyone needs is an upset ghost reliving its death over and over in your attic. Or, in this case, in your drunk tank. Thankfully, Will didn't turn around often.

"No, I don't have a date, Will, I came to see what you were up to."

He leaned back against the bars, his elbow sticking out between them. "Just tormenting the drunk. It's rather fun, care to join me?" He pointed at Mickey, who was now passed out, upright against the concrete wall with his mouth wide open and snoring.

"I'm sure it is Will, but he's pissing Ryan off with the yelling, which is making Ryan yell at me. Leave him alone, please? Or at least wait till Ryan's gone? Or me?"

He scrunched his handsome face. "Ooh, I hate Ryan. I'll leave the drunkard alone for you, my bonnie lass. But the moment you're gone, he's mine."

Smiling, I gave him a nod. "Thank you." I watched Will disappear, and I walked back to Moss's desk. Everyone's eyes were still on me. "He's gone!" I yelled louder than I needed to for Ryan to hear me in his office across the room. My Abuela would have scolded me for such unladylike behavior, but you can't be ladylike all the time. I sank back into the chair next to Moss's desk as chuckles surrounded us. "Okay, well, now that the daily 'Ryan yelling at me' is done, it's time to go home and see if I can find information about goo in any of my books."

"Sounds good. I'll walk you to your car." He stood up and took my coat off his coat rack, and held it open for me. Moss was an old-fashioned type of guy who opened doors for me and walked me to my car. Then again, it could also be a cop/safety deal since it was nighttime. Either way, I didn't mind. I slinked into my little black coat, and I caught a whiff of Moss's cologne. He always smelled good, low-key spicy with a hint of orange.

We walked into the morgue, which led to the parking garage, and saw Nicola putting her coat on.

"Leaving?" she asked.

"Yeah, gonna go read about goo!" I tried to sound excited about it, but it was difficult. I grabbed the takeout box with my bruschetta and could feel how cold it had gotten. *Aw, man.*

"Well, let me know what you find, I'm gonna get a cuppa." She took a step but whirled back to us. "Oh! Amelia's in the freezer. I forgot to tell you earlier and I don't like to bother her in there. Maybe mention the goo to her before you go?" She turned on her toes and left the morgue. I slowly turned to Moss, one hand on my hip. He was in trouble now.

"Amelia's here, isn't that interesting?" I asked, a plastic smile on my face.

"Is it?" I walked around him like a lioness stalking prey. The memory of fresh bruschetta was ruined by the sound of green goo jiggling on a metal table. Knowing the little crostini bread would now be soggy, it all made the situation even more annoying.

"Why call me...when Amelia...was already here? I was just about to take my first bite into my bruschetta." I opened the take-out box and showed him the pile of tomatoes, basil, and garlic on top of the now mushy bread. "The smell of tomatoes and garlic were already making my mouth water. When you call me to the morgue...when Amelia..." I poked him in the chest, "was already here."

"Sorry!" He put his hands up, trying to stifle a chuckle. "She didn't answer her phone. Does she usually spend time in the morgue?"

I sighed, annoyed, and laid my forehead on a nearby wall. "Yes, she likes it in there."

I heard his feet shuffle next to me. "Why?"

"She feels more connected to the dead than the living, and her husband doesn't want her to summon them in their house. So, she comes here." I spread my arms wide, my head still on the wall. "Cause it's dead central." I moved away from the wall, confident I now had a big red mark on my forehead, and closed my takeout box. I waved for him to follow me and started for the freezer. "Come on, let's go see if she's okay." I pulled open the door to what Nicola called the 'freezer.' It was where the dead waited for their families to sign them out.

Arion was a small town, so there were usually no more than three or four of the dozen slots filled at a time. That was enough for Amelia. She was indeed still in there at the other end of the room. She was sitting in a fold-out chair, wearing a coat and wool hat. It did tend to be a bit chilly in there if you're in there for longer than five minutes, and Amelia could be in there for hours. "Amelia?" I called out, and she quickly turned around.

"Lily! Sorry, you startled me." She turned back to the wall and waved her hands in the air to cancel her spell, and got out of the chair. The ghosts she summoned never showed up in person, just in her mind. I envied her for that on occasion. Like when I'm getting out of the shower. "What's up?"

"Just making sure you're okay before we go. How are the dead?" I asked.

"Still dead," Amelia said with a smile. She and her husband Jackson had a good ten years on me but didn't look it. They say doing what you love helps keep you looking young, which was true for them. But I swore I found a gray hair in my armpit last week.

That can't bode well for me. I'm barely thirty!

"Come here, I want to show you the most glorious green blob you're ever going to see." We started for the table where the blob still lay.

"So, it isn't another zombie cat ready to traumatize children?" she teased.

Moss snickered, and I shook my head. "Ha, ha. I knew I shouldn't have told you that," I said as she giggled. "Shall I tell them you feel like another dip in the town fountain? Nekid?" I pointed to the police officer's upstairs.

"Pft, that was fun, and you know it." She pulled out her cell phone. "Oh, crap, I missed a call. Who is Moss?"

"That would be me," Moss said. He looked over at me, a smug look on his face that said, 'I didn't need to be as snarky as I was' to him.

I shrugged. "Sorry, but if you had Intermezzo's bruschetta, you'd know I was justified!"

"Oh man, Lily, I'm sorry," Amelia said as she pulled the hat off her head, letting her tight curls bounce back to life. "If I had known, I would have paid better attention. I'll try harder."

"It's okay, Amelia, I get it." *I did get to see Detective Hotty for a while, so it wasn't all bad.* We stopped a few feet away from the table, and I pointed toward the exam tables. "Take a look at that." Amelia turned, and I watched her eyes go wide as they landed on the bowling ball of goo. "Weird huh? Never seen so much goo before. Or at all, really." Amelia turned around and took a step back towards the freezer. But her other leg took a step back towards the table. She looked like her body wanted to keep walking, but her brain was trying to talk her out of it. She took another step, then stepped back with both legs. It was an unusual looking dance. "What's wrong?" I moved out of her way in case her dance got even crazier.

"Where did you find that? When?" She was suddenly a little manic. It was surprising. Amelia was usually the calmer of the three of us. The goo really had her worked up.

"In an alley near Rosetree, about an hour ago," Moss said.

She turned and stared at me for a moment. Her huge dark eyes looked shocked. "An hour ago?"

"Yeah, were you here an hour ago?" I pointed back to the freezer.

She nodded manically. "Yeah, here, I was here an hour ago. Just an hour ago, yeah." I looked over at Moss. We both had the same 'what the hell is going on look' on our faces. "I'll see you later." Amelia waved and left us alone in the morgue.

"Wait, do you know," It was clear she didn't plan to stay. "What it is. Okay."

Moss walked up next to me, keeping an eye on Amelia. "She's not normally like that, is she?"

"No, she's usually pretty calm." I pulled out my cell phone and texted Jackson. *'Is Amelia doing okay? She seems a bit stressed.'* "We'll see if Jackson has any insight." Then I texted Amelia, hoping she'd see it eventually and get back to me. *'Do you know what the green blob is?'* I put the phone back in my pocket.

"Well, everyone has their off days," Moss said as we walked to the underground garage. It smelled like oil and burned rubber from police officers speeding away to emergencies. I watched as Amelia's red car sped out from the garage and turned onto the street. She really was in a hurry.

"True. Well, call me if you need me. If I find anything about the goo in my books, I'll let you know."

"I'd like to hear the title of that book." Moss held my car door open for me, and I slipped behind the driver's wheel.

"We'll see if I can even pronounce it." He shut the door, and I could hear him laughing. I liked making him laugh. To me, he seemed like a guy who liked to laugh but didn't have much reason to. Not sure if it was my witchy instincts or my womanly intuition that made me feel that way. But I'd be damned if I weren't going to make him laugh at least once whenever we saw each other.

CHAPTER SEVEN

I sat on my new black sectional, covered in my dark green blanket, going through the books I thought might have goo in them. Not in-in, just about goo, you know what I mean. But so far, I wasn't having any luck. I looked at my phone for the third time in half an hour, and there was still no reply from Jackson or Amelia. Either his phone was dead, or he was trying to help his wife. I knew he got uncomfortable when she spent more time in the morgue than at their house, but he had always worked through it with her.

I picked up a piece of toast that I covered with my bruschetta and was about to take a half-satisfying bite of tomatoes and garlic when my ear twitched. That was a hint an entity was trying to contact me. It happens more often than you'd think. You just have to pay attention. I quickly put the toast down and listened. I closed my eyes, and I could hear a faint voice calling out, but I couldn't quite understand what they were saying. I opened my eyes and snapped my fingers, lighting the tall, white candle I kept on my coffee table for just this reason. Most times, a ghost needed a little extra energy to come through, and it was better for it to take that energy from the fire instead of me.

"I know you're there, but I can't hear you. Can you use the flame?" I focused on the candle and watched it grow tall, then quickly go out. "Try really hard, speak loud, think loud!" I encouraged the entity and listened. *'elp. They have…apped, can't…'* I shook my head and strained to hear, but I was only getting bits and pieces, but I could tell it was male. *'…out. Please, Lily!'* His voice yelled my name, and my arms broke out in goosebumps.

"Do you know me?" It wasn't the best way to find out a friend I knew had passed, but it wouldn't be the first time it had happened. When I was in high school, I was watching a movie in the living room when the apparition of a boy who was a few grades below me walked into the room. His head was bloody, and part of his skull was missing. I remember screaming before he disappeared. The next morning, we learned he had died in a car accident, and I finally understood what I saw. I was more aware of my surroundings after that.

I strained to hear the voice again, but there was nothing. I lit the candle again, but it didn't budge. "I'll try my best," I said, in case he was listening. I looked over at my books and sighed. "Guess the goo's gonna have to wait."

***

My ringing phone woke me which startled me to attention. I immediately regretted it. Seems I had fallen asleep on the couch, and my neck was pissed about it.

I groaned and swiped right. "Yeah?" I croaked out.

"Lily? Are you okay?" It was Moss.

"Yeah, slept funny, what's up?"

I heard him sigh heavily. *"Your invisible friend is being particularly poltergeisty today. Major Ryan couldn't get ahold of Jackson or Amelia, so he wants you to come in and 'get rid of him,' his words, not mine."*

I sighed, stretching the sleep from my body. "Yeah, not doing that, but I'll be right there. Maybe I can get him to chill out."

"Great, see you in a bit." I swiped left and hung up to check my messages. Jackson hadn't even seen the one I sent him yesterday, but I had a text from Amelia. I gasped and quickly touched the icon. **It's not goo. It's headlining!** I growled and slapped my phone on my thigh, "Damn it, autocorrect, why do you have to be so dumb!" There was no way that's what she meant. I quickly pulled on a work-friendly button-down shirt and jeans and grabbed my silver bomber jacket. As

easygoing as Moss was, I didn't think he'd appreciate me showing up to work in polka-dotted boxers and a ripped t-shirt that was three sizes too big.

***

I walked into the bullpen from the garage elevator, but everything looked normal. I didn't see any sign that Will was misbehaving. Papers weren't strewn on the ground. No one was screaming about coffee spilling in their laps, nothing. I walked over to Moss and took a seat next to his desk.

"Seems awful quiet around here. Or did you just want to see me?" I teased. He laughed and sat back in his chair. It creaked like the old wooden thing it was.

"It's been that way for about ten minutes. He seemed upset before that." Moss sighed. "Never thought I'd say that about a ghost." He gave a little chuckle and leaned closer. "Seeing you is just a perk."

I managed to keep in my giggle but couldn't hide my smile. "You didn't have a ghost at your last job?" I was only halfway kidding, I didn't think all precincts had a ghost, but they do tend to attract the lost.

"Oh no, every time one showed up, the chief quickly got rid of it. He'd say, 'We deal with enough of that stuff out there. We don't need it here'."

"Hmm, I suppose that makes sense. Well, let me find him, see what I can do." Will loved making Nicola jump out of her fancy shoes, so I got up and started my search in the morgue. I walked down the stairs, and my shoes squeaked on the linoleum floor, making Nicola look up from her desk.

"Ahh, Ryan, call you in? I heard the commotion upstairs." I walked over and leaned on her desk.

"Will didn't come in here, did he?"

"Nope. Thought he would, too. The worst fit I've ever seen him have. You getting' rid of him?"

"Pft, no. He doesn't seem agitated now, I just need to find him, figure out what got him all riled up." I searched around the morgue but found nothing. It was eerily quiet. Back in the bullpen, it was the same, no ghostly activity. I didn't even get any weird feelings like I normally do around Will. His presence makes my skin break out in goosebumps, but my skin wasn't reacting to anything. Finally, I walked back into the holding area and found him. He was at the end of the hallway, staring up at the ceiling, not moving. His normal, excited puppy demeanor was gone. I don't think I've ever seen him so still. "Will?"

"Hey Lass." He didn't look at me. He just kept staring up. I followed his gaze, but there was nothing there. I closed my eyes and felt for any extra energy, but there was nothing. Will gasped, "Oh, didja see that!"

I quickly looked but saw and felt nothing. "No,

sorry, Will. What are you looking at?"

"Ya cannae see it? Oh, then we know it's bad." He was right, though. If I couldn't sense this thing he was looking at, it was bad. It was either too powerful for me to deal with or purposefully hiding from me. Neither of those situations was something I wanted to deal with alone.

"What's it look like? Can you describe it to me?"

"Not much to describe, really, a large black blob. In the corner up there." He pointed up at the ceiling, but there was nothing I could sense.

"Is that what made you throw a fit?"

"Aye, lass. I was hoping I could scare it off. Sometimes we get rogue spirits, and normally I can get 'em to go, but this...I don't know what this is."

"Do you think it'll hurt anyone?" I hated having to rely on his reckless attitude towards the people who worked here, but he was the only one I could ask.

"Hard to say. Oh! It looks like it's breathing! Aw, it stopped." My head whipped to the corner even though I knew I wouldn't see anything.

"Breathing?"

"Well, not actual breathing, looked like it was, though, just for a sec." Will moved his hands together and then apart a few times, mimicking the breathing he saw. I walked to that end of the room, but no matter what I did, I couldn't sense what Will could. "There it goes again, oh, it stopped."

"Weird. Well, can you do me a favor and stop throwing things around for a while? Ryan is getting close to wanting you gone, and I don't want to do that."

"Sure thing, Lass, I'll just keep an eye on this. Make sure it don't hurt nobody."

I chuckled at how seriously he was taking his new role. "Thanks, Will." After one more look into the empty corner, I walked back to Moss's desk and leaned in close so nobody could overhear me. "Will said there's something weird back there. His fit was him trying to scare it off."

Moss looked curious. "Isn't that nice of him. What's back there?"

I shrugged and sat back. "Not sure, I can't see it or sense it. It's something I've never encountered before."

"You don't think he's faking to get out of trouble, do you?" Honestly, I hadn't considered that. But knowing Will like I do, I don't think he'd act so protective unless something was truly there.

"No. He's worried, I can tell." Out of the corner of my eye, I saw Will walk into the bullpen, his eyes glued to whatever was on the ceiling. "He just walked in," I pointed towards the row of desks in front of Ryan's office. "He's still staring at something." I watched Will be more attentive than I've ever seen him. Normally when he walks, he still likes to move around objects, like living people do. But this time, he was walking through desks, chairs, and even people.

I reached up and fiddled with the crystal around my neck, it only took a second to realize something felt off. I lifted the crystal to my eyes. The smokey mist inside was gone, like the spell was being oppressed. I should have been able to sense the spell on it and see the wispy smoke, but there was nothing, no tingly feeling. I felt nothing from it. "Huh."

"Something wrong?" Moss asked. I looked back up to the ceiling where Will was still staring and decided to try something different. Looking for nothing was something one doesn't do, you look for something, anything. That little tingle of a spell or the smell of burnt offerings. But looking for nothing, that's tricky. I closed my eyes, and instead of concentrating on what Will was looking at, I focused on the area around what he was looking at, and Boom! I felt it. I could see the big dark blob in my mind's eye, undulating in the air. What a tricky, tricky person to have conjured such a spell.

"I think whatever Will's looking at is interrupting my magic."

Moss looked around, but I knew he wouldn't see anything either. "That doesn't seem good. Should we leave?"

"Yeah, we can test it." We got to our feet, and I concentrated on my crystal. It wasn't until I was outside the building that the magic returned to my crystal. We did this over and over, and I know we garnered looks, but testing takes time. As we stood outside, I came up with some hypotheses.

"All right, either my crystal is acting up, which I doubt, or that thing in there is blocking my magic."

"Like it doesn't want you to do magic?" Moss sounded worried.

"Seems like it. But to do that, that blob must be close, which means whoever is doing it must know where I am or where I'll be."

Moss's eyes narrowed. "Someone's magically stalking you?" His tone was angry and protective.

"Perhaps. My apartment is secure, though. I should be safe there."

"Maybe I can convince Ryan to give you a guard outside?"

I shook my head. "I doubt that, but I appreciate the thought." The crystal began glowing in pulses, and my arms broke out into goosebumps. "Damn it! Just when I say my apartment is safe." I held up my crystal, "This means someone broke in."

"Let's go." Moss and I ran back into the precinct, and the moment I did, my crystal stopped glowing, but I knew it was the blob interfering. "Moe, Karl, there's a burglary in progress at Ms. Roa's apartment. Come with us." He shouted at two uniformed officers who jumped from their desks and ran with us to the garage. I got in Moss's car, and he peeled out of the garage, the two other officers behind us. Like before, the farther away from the precinct, the brighter my crystal began to glow. It also started vibrating, which meant whoever broke in was still there.

"They're still in my apartment."

Moss reached for the radio and contacted the car behind us. "Suspect is still on scene. Prepare for a magical combatant."

"*Roger, Detective.*" It didn't take them long to get to my apartment with the lights and sirens on. They got a block away and turned the sirens off so as not to scare the intruder into leaving. Moss pulled in front of the building, and the other officers went around back. I lived on the third floor, and there was only one elevator, which Officers Moe and Karl took while Moss and I ran up the stairs. The elevator isn't the best, so I was used to trudging up the stairs. We got to the third floor, and my crystal was still pulsing.

"Still in there," I said quietly. Moss and I both ran as quietly as we could to my door, number seven. It was closed, but I could see the wood chipped around the lock and door frame. Moss pulled his gun but kept it pointing at the ground. The elevator dinged, and

Officers Moe and Karl stepped into the hallway and started for us.

"Get behind me," Moss said, "Moe, go non-lethal, Karl, back him up." They nodded and did as he said, pulling out a taser and gun, respectively. I noticed Moss looking at my crystal. It was still pulsing with light. He nodded, then slowly turned the doorknob. The door was silent as it swung open. No creepy haunted house squeaks from my door. I peeked around Moss and could see the door to my witchy room was open. I never left it open when I left the apartment.

"My witchy room," I whispered. Moss knew about my special room and moved into the apartment, gun still pointed at the floor. Moe went in after and started searching the right side of the apartment. Officer Karl went in and stood by the door, guarding, I assume. But this was my apartment, and I knew my little traps. I stepped around Officer Karl and held up my right hand.

"*Glacies*," I whispered, and my hand instantly became covered in frost. I heard Officer Karl gasp behind me. I tried not to worry about what he might think as I touched the wall of the coat closet behind the door. Frost quickly spread from my hand while Moss searched the apartment.

"Arion police, we know you're in here!" I watched the frost spread quickly along the wall onto the floor and over to the window across from me. "Come out with your hands up!"

The frost suddenly started climbing an invisible thing in my living room. It looked like legs. "Moss in here!" I yelled. I could hear someone reacting to the cold, and the frost quickly enveloped the invisible person. Moss pointed his gun at the intruder, and Moe ran to my side and pointed the taser at them. The frost-covered person stood with their hands up, their head turning to look at all of us.

"Get down on your knees and put your hands over your head!" Moss yelled, and Officer Kyle got out a pair of handcuffs. I felt the prickly sensation of magic and saw the person's hands were moving.

"Don't you even think of casting!" I formed a fist with my right hand and made the frost turn to ice. The person let out a yell while Officer Kyle grabbed their arms and pulled the person to the ground. The sound of ice cracking made the men cringe, but I knew it was just the ice around the person. They were fine. The handcuffs clicked shut, and Officer Moe called in to say that they were bringing in a burglary suspect.

"Why don't you have a look around, see if anything's missing," Moss suggested as he put his gun away.

"Sure." I closed my eyes and held out my hands, palms facing away from me. "Absens." You know that saying 'a place for everything and everything in its place'? What most don't realize is it's an old spell witches still do to keep track of their things. Dealing with cheeky spirits can sometimes result in things moving around, so it's a fantastic way to quickly check on your belongings. The spell swept through my apartment, but nothing was missing. Nothing was even out of place. "Everything's here. Nothing's wrong."

"That doesn't bode well." I heard Moss mutter.

"Why's that?"

He turned, putting his gun back in his hip holster. "If he wasn't here to burgle, why was he here?"

My eyes widened with shock. "You think he wanted to kidnap me?" Moss and Kyle both nodded at me. I knelt to the guy on the floor. "Were you going to kidnap me?"

"I'm not saying a word," he growled at me.

I gasped and got to my feet. "You're right, Moss. Of course, he was stupid to think I wouldn't show up without a cop. But why the hell would anyone…" Realization hit me like a truck. "Jackson and Amelia. It's been too long since I've heard from them."

Moss's head whipped up, his eyes as wide as mine. "Ryan said he couldn't get ahold of them this morning either. We have to go check on them. Officer Kyle, can you get this suspect to the precinct? We have two other possible missing witches we need to find."

"Yes, sir."

"Let me know what he says in interrogation." Officer Kyle nodded and heaved the now melting man to his feet. Officer Moe grabbed him by the other side of his arms and marched him from my apartment. "Are you sure nothing's missing?" he asked me again.

I nodded. "I'm sure." I did a quick walkthrough and looked with my eyes just to be extra sure, and nothing looked out of place. "The fact that he was invisible when he was in here just makes it even creepier. He really did want to take me, didn't he?"

"The fact that nothing's out of place and he was hiding supports that theory, along with the fact that we have two other missing witches in town. We need to go check their house. You know where they live, I assume?"

"Yeah, it's easy to get there."

CHAPTER EIGHT

Amelia and Jackson lived in the newer part of town, but the contractors took great strides to make sure the houses matched the town's aesthetic. Turn of the century seaside village is what ninety percent of the town looked like. I called both their cell phones while Moss drove, and both went directly to voice mail. Moss pulled up to their little house after heeding my directions, and everything looked normal. Their cars weren't in the driveway, which was the only thing that looked odd to me. They worked from home, running a monthly magical subscription service to supplement their income when they weren't working for the police. It was rare for both their cars to be gone.

"How long since you heard from them?" Moss asked as we got out of his car.

"Last I heard from Amelia was that text she sent overnight. Jackson, I haven't seen in about a week, but the last text I had from him was two days ago. They seemed fine, except for that little anxiety dance Amelia did in the morgue."

We walked up to the front door, and Moss rang the doorbell. "Do they have any family around here?" I could hear the doorbell inside the home but no footsteps on their creaky wooden floor.

"No, they're both only children, and their parents live on the East Coast, I think?" Moss rang the bell again, but no one answered. I knocked on the door, and it opened slightly.

"That's lucky." Moss pushed the door open a bit more.

"Yeah." I wasn't about to tell him I had permission to knock on their door to open it. A little witchy protection goes a long way.

"Jackson! Amelia! This is Detective Moss with the Arion Police. Are you here?" No answer. I peeked inside and saw their couch overturned, and the crocheted blankets that usually draped the back of it were ripped and scattered around the room.

"It does look like there was a scuffle in there." The television above the fireplace was also on the ground, smashed.

"I'm going to call this in. Stay out here just in case." I nodded, and he stepped back to his car to contact the precinct. I paced the front porch, rubbing my arms. I could feel the aura of a powerful spell inside, but like the spell at the precinct, I didn't recognize it.

Moss came walking back up to the porch, unbuttoning his suit jacket. "Since you haven't heard from them and the door is unlocked, we can go and check, but don't touch anything in case."

"Gotcha." I let him take point as he opened the door a little more with his foot.

"Arion police!" He announced our presence, and we walked inside. "Is anyone home?" I folded my arms against my stomach, trying to keep my 'touch everything' instinct in check. I walked to where I felt the unusual spell. It was at the end of the front hallway on the left. That was their witchy room. I had been in there so many times I could walk around with my eyes closed. I turned the corner into the hallway, and the spell in the back room went off. It messed with my equilibrium, and I couldn't stand straight. Step after step towards the room, I felt like I was moving through Jell-O. I reached the room, and everything happened so fast. I caught a glimpse of a completely empty room, covered in large blood splatters a second before I felt woozy.

"Ooh." I grabbed the door frame to steady myself, but my legs went wobbly, and I fell to the ground.

"Roa?" I heard Moss yell my name a second

before his face appeared above mine, but he was spinning.

"Get me out of here." I was proud that I managed to say that without vomiting. My stomach was roiling from the spell. Moss picked me up princess-style and ran from the house. Might have been fun if I didn't feel nauseated. When we got to the porch, I felt better. A total one eighty. "Oh, that was unexpected. And nasty."

"Are you okay?" He gently set me on my feet and held my face in his hands. I watched his eyes roam over me, looking for a sign of something wrong. "What was that?" His pretty eyes locked with mine, and the worry changed to something else, something soothing. His hands were warm, and they slipped down my cheeks to my neck, then my shoulders. It took everything in my being not to shiver.

"It was a spell in the back room. Felt like it didn't want any magic user going in there."

I heard sirens in the distance, the back up that Moss called for, no doubt. I blinked and took a step back, though I didn't really want to. "I know I'm not the most dependable in the house, but I could have sworn the entire room was covered in blood." I crossed my arms over my stomach. The thought that my friends were dead and that could have been their blood worried me. I never worry about my witchy friends. I didn't like that feeling.

Moss seemed to hesitate as he nodded. "There did seem to be a lot of blood." Police cruisers pulled up to the house, and my stomach dropped as I saw Major Ryan get out of the closest one.

"Oh shit. What the hell is he doing here?" I said, trying not to move my lips very much.

Ryan stomped up the stairs and stopped in Moss's face. "Moss, don't tell me you called in a missing persons alert for some witches."

"I did, sir. No one had heard from them, and I believe one or both had been critically injured. The back room-"

"You went in?" Ryan interrupted him.

"The door was unlocked, sir. And no one answered my yells." A few other officers came up to the porch, and one went into the house. The other stopped in front of me.

"Hey, Lily." It was Officer Mason. We grew up in the town together. Thankfully, he was one of the ones who just ignored me instead of being outwardly hostile.

"Mason."

He pulled out a little notebook and a pen. "So, what's going on?"

I sighed and leaned back against the house. "Well, I've been trying to get ahold of both Jackson and

Amelia since…"

"White!" Ryan barked at Mason, and we both jumped. "Don't take her statement. We're leaving."

"But—"

"No but's officer, let's go. Wherever they are, I'm sure they're fine. They're witches, right? We don't need to waste resources finding them."

"Pardon me, sir," I pushed away from the wall, "they're still missing people. Witches aren't indestructible. Sometimes, we need help." He walked up to me, much like he did the other day when Will was pissing him off.

"They're fine, Roa. They're witches, and they can manage whatever it is. They're on their own. Let's go." The way he said it, the uniformed officers knew they didn't have a choice. Mason closed his little notebook and put his pen away.

"Sorry," he mumbled, and the officers streamed off the porch.

"And you…" He pointed at Moss, "leave it alone, or I'll put you on street duty." Ryan turned, and we watched the few cars that came leave one by one.

"That son of a bitch," I said and started pacing. Moss stepped closer to me, and I felt his hands on my shoulders, stopping me.

"I'm not going to let this go, Lily. Something clearly happened, but we're not alone. One of the techs told me they took two vials of blood from that back room before they left. I guess they work faster than Ryan realized. He said he'd drop it off with Dr. Stroud."

I nodded. "Good idea." I noticed the door was still open. "I need a few more things. Wait here." Moss nodded and let me go back into the house. I could tell the spell was still there, waiting for me to peek into the room again, but maybe I could outsmart it? I pulled out my phone and opened the camera. I pressed against the wall and held my phone out in front of me. I inched little by little towards the doorway. When my phone could get a clear picture of the room, I felt dizzy, but not like earlier. I guess I wasn't close enough just yet. I snapped a pic and dashed to their bedroom on the other side of the house.

When the wooziness was gone, I looked at the picture. It was clear enough that I could indeed see the empty room was covered in blood. "Perfect." I went into their bedroom and grabbed a pair of earrings off the dresser that I knew Amelia wore almost every day. On the floor (of course), I saw a t-shirt of Jackson's with a chicken on it and picked it up. When I walked out of the house, Moss stopped pacing and shut the door behind me.

"Find anything?"

I opened my photo gallery and showed him the

picture of the room I had taken. "Like I said earlier, this is their witchy room."

Moss looked at me, confused. "It looks empty."

"Exactly."

"Are you telling me all their spell components and books are gone?" He had seen my witchy room, so he knew it could be full of herbs, books, and shelves. But this room was empty, except for the blood on the walls and floor.

"Looks that way."

Moss shook his head in annoyance. "This much blood in a house, and Ryan ignores it?"

"To be fair, I don't think he saw it or anyone told him about the amount of blood."

Moss snickered. "You have every right to be angry at him, yet you defend him. You got a big heart, Roa."

I smiled. "More like a big brain." I sat on the swing they had on the porch. "I don't know how many times I complained about Ryan over the years. Nothing ever happens. Not even Howard could get us justice. Since we're just consultants, we don't seem to matter much."

"Well, you matter to me." I could hear the passion in his voice, how much he agreed that the way Ryan treated us was unfair. But Howard felt that way too, and if a thirty-year veteran couldn't change anything, what could a guy who had been here less than a year do?

"Thanks, Richard."

He gave one nod. "You bet."

I started pacing again. It helped me think. "It takes balls to steal from a witch's conjuring space, not to mention the entire room." I sighed and ran my hands through my hair and figured this mystery needed a ponytail. "Okay," I quickly grabbed a hair tie from my back pocket and tried to tame my mane. My hair being the way it was, untamable and thick, I had hair ties stashed everywhere. Pockets, cars, Nicola even had half a dozen stashed away for me. "If I were going to kidnap a pair of witches...I'd be insane. There's no way anyone would be so stupid to try and get two of us at the same time. Unless there were a lot of people with me." I gasped and turned back to Moss. "Or I got one at a time," I said, pointing at him.

Moss walked off the porch to examine the front lawn. "Well, the grass doesn't seem like it's been trampled. Since Amelia texted you, and Jackson didn't, maybe they grabbed Jackson first and...Amelia found them in their house, and they got the better of her?"

"Possibly." It was starting to look grim for my friends.

"Can you do that same spell you did at Howard's house?" Moss asked. That spell let me see what happened in the last few hours of a victim's life. We were able to see Howard and his wife running from the creature that killed them. The spell could be handy, but not today.

I shook my head. "I wish. I need to be inside, and there's no way I can concentrate enough to pull it off with that weird spell on the back room."

"Damn." Moss came back up on the porch and stood in front of me.

I groaned and covered my face with my hands. "Oh, man." I sniffed and lowered my hands. "All right. I need to find Amelia and Jackson, but since their witchy room was raided, I need mine."

"All right. Need your faithful Igor?" I had dubbed him Igor when he was helping me with Howard's case, but thankfully, he didn't take offense. I was still surprised at how he didn't freak out at all the magic that happened around us that day.

"Absolutely."

CHAPTER NINE

I paced around my witchy room in my apartment, trying to decide what I needed to find my friends. I had plenty of herbs, crystals, and scrying mirrors to pick from, but I needed to be accurate. The mirror might only show me them, not their surroundings, and crystals tended to not work as effectively the further away you got from where you cast the spell. For this, I needed a map. Thankfully, I had one on my sticky board and laid it on the refurbished morgue table next to Amelia's earrings and Jackson's shirt. For the herbs, I decided on frankincense for a little bribe to the spirits and peppermint for a little mental boost.

"Is this you?" I turned and saw Moss pointing to a picture I kept in my witchy room of me and my family. I was three, so it was about a year before they all died. My Abuelo was holding me upside down, so my huge smile looked like a horrible frown. I loved that picture.

"Yep. Cinco-de-Mayo at my Tia's house. Last one I spent with them."

"Your grandparents?"

I looked over at him. "My entire family."

His eyes went from curious to full of sympathy. "Oh, gosh, I'm sorry. I didn't realize when you said your family was gone. You meant all of them."

"It's all right. It was a long time ago. Can you get that mortar and pestle for me and put it on that table?" I pointed to the tools on the second shelf behind him.

He quickly did as I asked. "Looks different in here." He said, turning around and eyeing the place.

The room was filled with shelves that held my ingredient jars. A mix of glass, tin, and old coffee cans. The wall with the window had a mismatch of other materials I might need, crystals, a wand or two made of different woods, and different colored ribbons. You never know what you might need, so I tended to stock up on everything I could get my hands on. The wood floor was covered in protection runes and alarm spells that I had to disarm before I walked in. Last time Moss was here, I was drying about a metric ton of herbs, and they made the room look tiny as they hung from the ceiling.

"All the herbs are in jars now," I said, pointing to the ceiling.

"Ah, I wondered why I wasn't walking around hunched over. You grow your own herbs?"

"I just dry them. Living in an apartment puts a damper on gardening." I put the frankincense and peppermint in the mortar and quickly got the remnants off my fingers. "I get a lot from Amelia and Jackson." I stopped as my eyes landed on the alarm spell on my floor. "Amelia taught me that." I pointed at the spiraling rune, and Moss walked over to me and looked down at the spell. "She said, 'You never want an uninvited guest in your conjuring space.' I always put a spell on my apartment and thought that was enough, but Amelia said, 'Oh no, some bad magic users are tricky. You want to protect everything.'"

"That crystal around your neck, was that for your apartment and here, or just your apartment."

"Apartment," I picked up the crystal. "I think they opened the door, saw the runes, and decided not to go in. If they had come in here, they'd be running around screaming with worms for arms." I looked up at him. "I still haven't heard back from anyone about that guy who broke in. Did he ever say what he was looking for?"

"No, last I checked, he still wouldn't talk. I can check now if you want?"

I shook my head. "Naw, that's okay, this is more important."

Moss walked around the sigil on the floor. "What would happen if an uninvited guest went into Amelia and Jackson's witchy room?"

"Well, depends on the witch. I suppose if you're creative you could get the spell to do whatever you wanted. But I never asked."

Moss slowly turned to me, his hand on his chin. "What if an uninvited person came into your room, and the runes made everything in the room disappear? Is that too crazy?"

My eyes went wide. "No, that's genius! Keeps your stuff safe and out of the hands of those who would use it to do harm! What if no one took their stuff, but it was transported to a safe place?" I paced a little and chewed on my lip. "Let's see, if Amelia ran into her room, she'd have to disarm the spells." I sighed, annoyed that my theory wasn't working out. "Then anyone could come in. That wouldn't work."

Moss scratched his nose in thought. "Well, what if they hurt her before she got into the room? Would the spell act the same? There was a lot of blood in the room, but I saw a few drops outside in the hallway. She could have gotten hurt before she went into the room. Maybe even by seconds."

I put my elbows on my table and laid my head in my hands. "The Fells were better witches than I am, I bet they had a contingency that if they were hurt, everything would disappear. They'd know how to bring everything back, so it wouldn't be an issue for it to disappear on them." I started digging in my pocket for my phone. "That might do it." I studied the picture more, and it looked like there was nothing in the room before the blood went everywhere.

"There's no streaks on the floor either." I jumped, not realizing that Moss was looking over my shoulder.

"Sorry," he chuckled. "I assume there are spells to transport people?"

"Mmm, yeah, but they're tricky. Not a lot of people use them." I put my phone back in my pocket and sighed. "If these are the same people who conjured that weird spell at the precinct, they're powerful, tricky, and most likely dangerous."

"I know nothing about magic, and I'm going to agree with you on that. Do you have any idea where the contents of their room might be?"

I shook my head and leaned back against the table. "No." I watched Moss drum his fingers on a nearby shelf before he hit a few buttons on his phone.

"Hey, Hyde, can you do me a favor?" Hyde was one of the newer officers. I didn't get to know him much before the townies got to him. "Can you do a little digging and find out if Jackson or Amelia Fell had a storage space in town?" I nodded. A big enough storage space could hold it all, but it might be packed in tight. "Thanks, let me know what you find. And make sure Ryan doesn't find out. Yeah, thanks." He hung up and put his phone back in his pocket. "Officer Hyde's going to check on storage units for us."

"Good idea. Wonder how long it'll take." I sighed and picked up Jackson's shirt off the table, and handed it to him. "In the meantime, can you rip off a piece of this shirt for me?" He pulled out a pocket knife from his pants and cut out the chicken that was printed on it. "Now no one will know 'what'!" I teased as I took the chicken from Moss. He laughed, and just the sound of it made me feel better. "Okay, into the cauldron chicken butt." I set the dangly blue earrings, shirt piece, and a bit of charcoal in the stone bowl next to the map of Arion.

"I thought that was a pestle?" Moss asked.

"Anything can be a cauldron, it just depends on if a fire is needed. Plastic bowls and lit charcoal don't mix." Moss nodded. It was nice that he was so curious and understanding. Made it more fun to work with him. "Hopefully, this will tell me where Jackson and Amelia are, so don't...freak out, okay?"

Moss's curious face flashed worry for a moment. "I've seen you draw a happy face with your own blood on a little bag of herbs, and _now_ is when you tell me not to freak out?"

I shrugged and nodded. "Yeah." I was about to snap my fingers and light everything up when my phone began ringing. "Argh." Annoyed, I took it out of my pocket but quickly calmed down when I saw it was Nicola. "Hey." I put it on speaker- phone so Moss could hear what she said too.

"*Hey Lil, so you know how you're always telling me I need to expand my horizons?*"

I could picture her doing air quotes at the end of the sentence. "Yeah?"

"*Well, I don't do goo, I don't do weird creatures, I do humans. So, I started treating the goo like a person.*" My eyes went wide as my lips disappeared into my mouth, trying to hold back a laugh. I tried to push the image of her telling a family made of goo how their fellow goo had died. '*Sorry, they were in the sun too long. They never had a chance.*'

"Oh?" I managed to say. If she heard me teasing, that'd be the end of her dabbling in the weird.

"*Yeah, so I gave the goo a blood test.*" Moss and I looked at each other, equally impressed. I never would have thought of that.

"Neat! Find anything?" I crossed my arms over my stomach and leaned against the table.

"*Well, it seems to have O-negative blood or remnants of O-negative antibodies in it.*"

"Weird, wonder what that means?" Moss looked

up at me with a shrug. I guess I'd have to depend on Nicola for the medical stuff.

"*I have a theory.*" She sounded excited. It was endearing. I always wanted her to get more interested in the preternatural world. Maybe this had done it?

"Please." Nicola cleared her throat, and I knew she didn't want to sound crazy, but she clearly forgot who she was speaking to. I'd never think that.

"*What if the goo…really was a person? I know you were just kidding earlier, but it got me thinking, and now I can't let it go.*" Moss and I looked at each other. He looked as worried as I felt.

"It's possible. I don't know how anyone would get turned into goo, though. Oh! That reminds me, you wouldn't happen to have the results of the blood that was taken from Jackson and Amelia's house, would you? We wanted to keep it quiet, so I wasn't sure how long it would take."

"*Let me check.*" I could hear sympathy in her voice as her fingers flew across the keyboard. "*I'm so sorry, Lily, I hope they find them.*"

"I'm about to cast a spell to find them now. Major Asshat was useless at their house."

Nicola groaned. "*Wanker. He thinks he can get away with anything.*" I could hear her typing furiously on her computer. "*Okay, so we don't have a match yet, but they've determined it's A-positive.*"

"That could be anybody," I said, "Are they still working on it?"

"*Yeah, the file is still unlocked.*" There was another loud clack of her keyboard. "*Huh,*" she said.

"What?"

"*Nothing, hopefully, it's just…according to Jackson and Amelia's file, his blood type is O-negative, and hers is A-positive.*"

I covered my mouth in shock, and Moss laid a hand on my shoulder. "That's not good."

"*I agree. If Amelia does show up here, I'll let you know.*"

"Thanks." I swiped left and put my phone back in my pocket. "I sure hope what I'm thinking isn't true."

"What are you thinking?" Moss squeezed my shoulder reassuringly.

I groaned and leaned against the table. "That the goo is Jackson, and Amelia is in a lot of trouble."

His face turned into a mix of confusion and 'gross.' "What?"

"Yeah. I don't understand how it would be him, but we'll worry about that later. Right now, let's see if we can even find them." I smashed the ingredients in the mortar a few times before I snapped my fingers, and in a flash, a fire burned the herbs, t-shirt, and earrings. I leaned over the smoke and breathed in frankincense and peppermint. I focused on Amelia and Jackson. I wanted to find them, I needed to know where they were, and I put that 'want' and intention into my spell and breathed the smoke onto the map. I liked doing this spell. It made me feel like a fancy dragon breathing smoke on stuff. But it was also a sad spell because it meant a person was missing.

I watched two smoke trails swirl around the map, searching the town of Arion for my fellow witches. One trail settled on the corner of Rosemund and Fifth. The other settled on the edge of the map at the Eldred Mansion.

"Does that mean they're in two different places?" Moss pointed at the map.

I sighed, staring at the little smokey blobs. "Looks that way. What's at Rosemund and Fifth?" I pulled my phone out and used the map app to see the business in the area. "Moss, you're not going to believe this." I held out my phone so he could see.

"Mark and Son's storage." He read aloud. He quickly pulled out his phone and called Officer Hyde. "Hyde, check out Mark and Son's storage. We have a lead." He hung up and looked back at the map. "So, what's there?" He touched the edge of the map where the smoke had stopped.

"The Eldred Mansion. No one's lived there for about twenty years."

He turned and leaned against the table, his arms crossed over his stomach. "Your typical haunted mansion I take it?"

"Yep. The family was murdered, and they never found the culprit. I was ten. I remember it being a big deal, but again, I was ten and more concerned with my Pokémon cards. Or lack thereof."

"Well, a crime like that is unnerving for a small town."

"But who is at the storage unit, and who is at the mansion?" I asked aloud. "The spell isn't that specific since I looked for both at the same time. Shouldn't have done that. Oh well, that's what desperation does to me. It makes me move too fast."

"You aren't the only one, Roa. Let's start with the storage unit. Maybe Hyde will find something." Moss started for the door.

"Good plan." I took two steps away from the table when I heard a loud pop behind me. Of course, I wasn't expecting it, and I screeched like a startled owl, but who wouldn't? Moss was a bit more professional. He turned, his hand on his sidearm as he pulled me back into the living room by my waist. We searched around us, but all we saw was a little puff of smoke hanging in the air above the map. Nothing else seemed to be out of place.

"What was that?" Moss finally let me go,

convinced nothing was going to hurt me.

"I…don't know," I walked back into the room and didn't see anything odd. "Maybe it was part of the…" I looked up and saw the puff of smoke was still there. It wasn't dissipating. "That's weird," I said to myself.

"Part of the weird? Yeah, I'll say," Moss said.

"Bah!" I waved my hand at him, "That's not what I meant. Look at this." I pointed at the smoke. "It's not moving." My ear twitched, and I gasped. "Oh shit!" I ran from my witchy room, arms flailing wildly to keep my balance as I ran around Moss and an end table in the living room. I snapped my fingers, lighting the candle on the table. "I know you're there!" I yelled.

'No! Stop loo…t…erous! Order of the Elements!' My ear popped, and I knew the spirit was gone. It sounded male, like it did the night before, but I still couldn't tell if it was Jackson. The voice was just too quiet.

"Order of the Elements," I said to myself. "Where have I heard that?"

"Graceful exit." I jumped as Moss walked up behind me. I almost forgot he was there.

"I'm like a cat." I playfully clawed the air as I leaned back against my couch.

"A cat with three legs."

I playfully slapped his chest as he smiled at me. "Yesterday, I heard a voice while I was researching the goo. Nothing unusual, it happens every so often, but I think it wants me to stop looking. If it means Jackson and Amelia or searching what the goo means, I'm not sure."

"Well, now, we can't do that." He held up the little notebook he kept in his jacket pocket. "Here's what the smoke made." I took the notebook and stared at the big symbol Moss drew on the page.

"The smoke made all that?"

"Yeah, you had to stand at just the right angle to see it, but you ran out to, uhh, speak to a ghost, I guess. So, I kept looking at it."

"Well damn, you are a good detective." I glanced at the notebook, it looked like a game of tic-tac-toe, but instead of x's and o's, it had five different symbols on it, four in the corners and one in the middle. "Okay, let's see if we can find Jackson or Amelia at the storage place. If we find their witchy room there, I bet we can use it to help us figure out what's going on. Their collection is quite extensive." I handed him his notebook back.

Moss gave a nod and put it back in his jacket pocket. "Sounds like a plan."

***

Moss pulled up to the gated facility of Mark and Son's storage and stopped by a number pad that you could punch numbers from in your car. It didn't really look like anyone was there to help us, either.

I sighed. "Now what?" Moss took his phone out of his pocket and reached out the window.

"Two, eight, six, four."

"All right, whose ass did you pull those numbers from?" The gate opened with a screech. "Nice."

"Hyde gave them to me. Said it's his own code to get in. Convenient, eh?"

"Indeed." He pulled into the parking lot but made sure it was far from the road. No need to make it easier on whoever these people were. We got out, and I put a little bit of ash from the chicken butt shirt and Amelia's earrings on the hood of the car.

"Still don't know what unit to look for," Moss said as he put his phone up.

"That's okay. It helps that we're in the area." I snapped my fingers, and the ash caught fire. I quickly breathed in the smoke like before and breathed it out, thinking about my friends. The smoke formed a line and started floating in the air towards the storage units.

"Handy," Moss said.

I coughed, and a little cloud of smoke puffed out of my mouth. "Yep." We followed the smoke for eight rows, and at unit number ninety-seven, it dissipated. I knocked on the garage door. "Jackson! Amelia! Are you in there? It's Lily, and I have Detective Moss with me! Open up!" My knocking turned to banging when no one answered.

"The spell worked, right?" Moss asked.

I sighed and stepped back a bit. "Yeah, it worked, but now what?" Moss looked around before pulling a little black bag out of his jacket pocket. He stepped up to the padlock on the unit and started picking it. I couldn't stop the smile on my face. "Detective, my, my, such skills you have!"

I saw the little dimple in his left cheek as he chuckled."Well, I wasn't always a cop." The padlock popped open, and he flung the garage door up. The storage unit was filled with the items from Jackson and Amelia's conjuring room. It looked like it was laid out like it was in the house, just squished together.

"I owe you a drink, Moss," I patted his back, "I can't believe it. Everything's here!"

"Yeah, but I don't see either of our missing witches." We slowly walked inside, ducking under stacked up chairs and moving around tables. It was dark inside, but I saw Moss hold up his hand. "Do you smell that?" I took a big sniff, and a strong metallic scent hit my nose.

"Blood." I looked up and found a pull chain for the lightbulb and pulled. Light filled the room, and I gasped. Blood was splattered on everything in the unit. "Oh my god." I looked at Moss and saw blood all over his white shirt. I held up my arms and saw the silver arms of my jacket were smeared with red. "What the hell is going on? Amelia! Jackson!"

"I don't see anyone in here." Moss was straining to look around the crowded space. "Why would the spell bring us here if they weren't here?" he asked.

I held up my blood-covered hand. "The amount of blood was enough to attract the spirits, it seems." I sighed.

"I'm sorry, Lily," Moss said and laid a hand on my shoulder but quickly took it off when he realized it was also covered in blood.

"We just need to find them, alive or dead. Preferably alive." I looked around and spotted their large bookcase towards the back of the space. "Moss, let me see that picture you drew." He tried wiping his hands off before pulling out his notebook, but it just smeared on his pants. With a groan, he carefully took the notebook out and flipped to the page before handing it to me. "There's got to be something in here that'll help."

"If blood hasn't ruined it." He started moving stuff out of our way, so we had a little room. Emphasis on little. I stared at the odd tic-tac-toe game he drew but only recognized one symbol. The one in the middle was a spirit. He drew a ghost (bless his heart). The rest, it seemed, were at the mercy of Moss's imagination.

"What's this one?" I pointed to the one in the

top left corner.

"That one looked like a mountain."

I looked up at him, my eyebrow raised. "So, you drew a boob with the nip pointing up instead?"

He laughed. "Trust me, if I drew a boob, you'd know it."

"Oh really? Okay, Monet, what's this one?" I pointed to the one in the top right corner.

"Uhh, it was a…tree or flower blowing in the wind." I looked at the picture and it mostly looked like a stick figure at a rave. "This one was clearly a campfire." He pointed at the one in the lower left corner.

"Campfire, aka, fuzzy clown wig, gotcha, and this one?"

The one in the lower right looked like a shower curtain to me. "Waterfall," he said.

"Oh! I can sort of see that!" I said enthusiastically.

"Yeah?" He looked up at me with a smile on his face.

"No, not one bit." He snickered and shook his head. "But I appreciate the effort, I would have missed this if you weren't with me."

"Faithful Igor, at your service." I smiled at him. Those little brown specks in his eyes were getting bigger, but we had more pressing matters to worry about.

"Okay, and this one is Spirit." I took the notebook and started to pace. Well, I tried to anyway. I quickly realized I had no room to pace, so I leaned on a nearby desk. "Mountain, blowing flower, campfire, waterfall, and spirit?" I said to myself over and over until it finally hit me. "They're elements, Order of the Elements," I whispered.

Moss moved over and looked at the notebook. "The order of them matters?"

"No, not the order, The Order, big 'O'," I looked up and held back a little squeal when I realized Detective Hotty was so close I had almost bumped into him. "The voice in my apartment was telling me to stay away from the Order of the Elements, while this shows up in the smoke while I was scrying for Amelia and Jackson. The mountain is Earth, the rave is Air, Fire, Water, Spirit, get it? It took me a minute to remember where I heard that name before. It's a cult, like the Illuminati of the preternatural world. And I think they have Amelia and Jackson at the Eldred Mansion." Moss just stood still and listened to me rant about my theory. His pupils were getting bigger as he stared at me.

Finally, he nodded. "Sounds plausible as anything. What is this Order?"

I put the notebook into the pocket of his coat jacket. "It's said they have their hands in everything from dragons to zombies. Others say they don't exist.

But I have a feeling they're real, and they're powerful." My eyes scanned the unit until I saw what I needed. "Help me move this stuff, I need those books." The biggest bookshelf was against the far wall of the unit, and there was a great deal of stuff between us and it. We rolled chairs and moved desks and boxes for a good fifteen minutes before I could get in front of the shelf. "Help me find my friends," I whispered to my right hand, "help me find The Order," and I ran my finger over the spines of the books I could reach. The tingle from the spell in my fingers told me I was close, but no cigar.

"Can you get me a chair to stand on? I need to check the ones on the top." Moss rolled over a chair and held it still while I climbed up. The books up here were thick, old, and dusty. I could tell I was closer, but still no prize. "I know I'm close, but these aren't it."

"What about on top of the bookcase?" I stretch every inch of my five-foot-two frame, but I still can't feel anything.

"I can't reach enough of it."

"Here." He let go of the chair and grabbed my legs around my knees. "Keep your legs straight, okay." He lifted me up a few more inches, and low and behold, I felt a book up there.

"I feel something!" A tingle spread through my arm, and I knew this was it and managed to grab it. "Okay, I got it." I thought he would just set me on the ground, but instead, I found myself sliding down his body. It didn't take long before I was face to face with the most handsome detective I've ever known. "Thanks."

"No problem." He smiled, and I realized my feet were already on the ground. I cleared my throat and put the book I grabbed on a nearby desk. Unlike most of the books on that shelf, this one had no dust on it. "I take it there won't be dog ears telling us exactly what we want to know?" he asked.

"Don't blaspheme. Bookmarks, or you deserve to lose your place." I scoffed. "Dog ears." I fought not to smile as he snickered. I looked at the top and saw a nice velvet bookmark that was built into the book. "This is how non-plebeians mark their books."

He shook his head as he chuckled. "Whatever that means."

I gently opened the book where the mark was, and I felt my fingers go numb. "Oh no."

"Oh no, what? Are you all right?" I lifted my hands to my face. The numbness went down to my wrists.

But it was just an echo of a spell, which was still bad. "Spells last as long as you want or until the person who cast them dies." I looked over at Moss, "Jackson or Amelia cast a spell on this book, but whoever cast the spell on the book...is dead." I felt his hands on my arms. "I can't tell who, but I have a feeling we're going to find a dead body before the day is through." I wiggled my fingers, and I could once again feel my hands. I could also feel my heart breaking at the thought of losing a close friend.

"I'm sorry, Lily. Can you tell what kind of spell it was?"

I took a breath and finally looked at the pages of the book. "No, when a spell dissipates because of death all you can feel is the remnants of magic, no markers to indicate what it was." I ran my finger around the page, and things started making sense. "It looks like one or both of them were looking into The Order." I moved aside so Moss could read as well. "The Order of the Elements was an old fraternal order of witches gathered from the most talented of the age. At first, it seemed all they wanted was to share knowledge, until one day in 1243, the leader, whose name was lost to history, declared those without magic unworthy."

"It's like a bad movie," Moss said.

"Where do you think they get the ideas for those bad movies. I should be a screenwriter." I kept reading, "After the failed coup, the group went underground. It's said they've had their hand in the greatest magical phenomena of the time, to when the dragon Amet rose in 1630, and when an entire village in France turned into undead without dying in 1879."

"I'm assuming it takes a great deal of power to do stuff like that?" I felt Moss's hand on my back as he leaned over and read with me.

"An insane amount." I turned the page, and my eyes widened as I saw Moss's drawing in the book. Albeit a much better representation of the elements since there were no boobs. "Look." I pointed to the drawing, and I heard Moss sigh.

"Yeah, that looks a lot better than what I did." His hand moved up to my shoulder. "Now what?" I wondered if he was giving me those touches because he thought I'd like them or that I might fall apart at any moment. But I wasn't going to fall apart, not yet, anyway.

"I think we should go to the mansion." I turned to him, he was still so close I couldn't help but glance at his lips. I'll admit, it was incredibly tempting, but we had missing witches to find. "The other smoke trail led there. Maybe we'll have more luck."

"Right, so we'll need backup?" We made our way out of the storage unit, and I helped him shut the door.

"Honestly, I think Amelia and Jackson were our backups."

He grimaced and locked the padlock. "Shit." We quickly walked back to his car. "I'll call Hyde back.

Maybe he can get a few volunteers."

"Just don't let Ryan hear, he'll bust you down to street cop, and it'll be my fault."

"It'd be worth it if we're right," he said.

I smiled at his determination. "And if we're not, and Ryan finds out?"

He shrugged. "Then you're getting a roommate." I laughed and took off my blood-covered jacket. "Deal, *purus*." The blood disappeared, and I did the same spell on the rest of our clothes. There was plenty in the storage unit for testing. Besides, I doubt Moss would appreciate the inside of his car smelling like blood. My stomach growled, and I remembered I hadn't eaten anything today. It was almost three in the afternoon. Damn it. "But first, as much as I hate to admit it, I need food. I just realized I forgot to eat breakfast. I'm no good on an empty stomach."

"That's fine. It gives us something to do while waiting to hear back from Hyde."

CHAPTER TEN

Since it was after the lunch rush, we didn't have to wait to get a seat at the greasy spoon called Sal's, down the street from the storage facility. It was the kind of place that had duct tape covering rips that jerky customers would make on purpose and floors that always seemed sticky. But they served breakfast all day and had the best biscuits and gravy, so I could forgive them.

I got a double order of them, and Moss got a tuna melt and fries. After the server left, we sat silently in the booth for a few minutes. My mind was racing with horrible scenarios that my friends might be in. I felt so guilty just sitting, waiting for food when they could be in danger. My stomach was fluttering with more than just hunger, and my foot was jiggling with nerves.

Moss's foot gently stopped mine from tapping. "You feel guilty, don't you?" Moss finally said. I looked up from my hands but didn't say anything. "About eating when your friends are out there, possibly in trouble." Man, he hit the nail on the head with that one. I licked my bottom lip and ran my hands over the condensation that had formed on my glass of water.

"How'd you know?"

"Detective trait." He had taken his suit jacket off and laid it next to him in the booth. I finally noticed his tie. It was black with tiny ghosts all over it. Could he be more perfect?

"A trait? Like you looked at me and concluded?" I teased.

He chuckled. "No. I remember the first case I worked as a rookie in Oregon. This poor old man had been beaten by his son and had his medication and money stolen. My partner was so sure since we knew who attacked the victim, it'd be an easy case. We'd find his son, charge him, etc. But as we leaned against the outside wall of a grocery store with our fish tacos, I found I couldn't eat."

"You wanted to find the guy."

Moss nodded. "I did. If we knew who it was, why not start the search? But my partner said, 'We're no good to anyone if we don't take care of ourselves.' That means eating and sleeping."

I rested my head in my hands. "Yeah. That makes sense. Did you find him?"

"Oh yeah," he said with a smile, "my partner was right. We found him in his own apartment high as a kite. It was an easy grab." A shadow fell across the table, and I looked out of the big window next to us. Mrs. Metcalf was staring at me through the window, her usual disappointed frown on her face. I rolled my eyes and tried to ignore her, but her shadow never moved.

Moss knocked on the window with a knuckle. "Move on, ma'am!" She didn't give him a second glance before walking away. "What's her problem? Are they out of her Nicorette gum at the pharmacy?"

I snickered, glad that Moss had a sense of humor. "Not a lot of people in town like me. Especially the older crowd."

Moss leaned forward. "You've alluded to that before. I don't get it. Why? Everyone grows up knowing about magic and monsters. Why don't they treat you better?"

I sat back against the duct tape-covered booth. "I'm a witch, I don't fit in, and hell, according to them, all the bad stuff is my fault. Only magic could bring such heartache!" I said dramatically.

He scoffed and shook his head. "That's ridiculous!"

I nervously licked my lips and decided to just tell him. I leaned forward against the table, my hands fiddling with my fork. "Well...they also think I killed my family."

Moss stared at me for a moment before he reached out and took my hand. "How could anyone think that of you?" His tone made my heart beat faster. No one had spoken so gently to me before.

I shook my head and squeezed his hand. "I don't know. I wasn't even home. Hell, I was four years old! But that didn't stop the rumors." The server brought our food, and I stopped talking and sat back, letting go of his hand. I didn't recognize her, so I doubted she knew of my dubious past, and I wanted to keep it that way for as long as I could.

"Let me know if you need anything else!" She left with a smile. I felt my mouth water as the smell of the biscuits and gravy reached my nose. The biscuits were big, flakey, and buttery, and the white gravy was creamy and perfectly peppery with the right amount of sausage chunks. I used my fork to cut a piece off, and steam filled the air.

"Can I ask what happened?" I looked up and Moss was chewing on a fry. I took a bite, and the hot gravy and buttery biscuit calmed me. They don't call it comfort food for nothing.

"I was at daycare when it happened. My mom dropped me off at the usual time. But no one came to pick me up, and even as young as I was, I knew something was wrong."

"Who took you home?" I watched him maneuver around the melt, trying to get a bite without dropping mayo on his shirt. It was cute.

"The owner. She was a family friend, so it wasn't unusual. She'd done it before. I remember she turned the corner to my street, and we were blocked by fire trucks and police cars. We parked as close as we could and started walking, but then the crime scene tape stopped us. I remember looking up at one point, the daycare owner had her other hand over her mouth, and she was shaking. But I was too short to see much. Another neighbor started pointing at me and an officer came over and talked to her. Next thing I knew, I was being whisked away to the police station. They were nice, and they gave me chicken nuggets and a teddy bear." I took a few more bites of my lunch. I needed more comfort in my stomach.

"After a few hours, a lady from CPS came and told me what happened. She said my house was destroyed in the fire, and everyone inside had died. My entire family happened to be over at the time, including all my aunts and uncles, and close cousins. I was the only one not there. They were getting ready for my uncle's birthday party, and my mom didn't want me underfoot, so she took me to daycare that day. I learned later that the fire was so hot and fast that no one could have escaped."

Moss clicked his tongue in a sympathetic manner. "Oh man, I'm sorry."

I waved him off. "It's okay, it was a long time ago." I sighed. "Anyway, I was bounced around the system for a few months until the one cousin who didn't live in town came and took custody of me. I don't really think she wanted to. She lived in California and moved here, so I didn't have to leave the only town I knew. But none of the safe houses wanted me to stay with them, and the city was running out of places to put me. See, the night before the fire, the old man across the street saw me in the front yard and told the police officers I was playing with matches and making fireballs with my mind." I looked up at Moss, and the 'Are you serious' look on his face was refreshing. "Yeah, I know, right? I had power when I was young, but it wasn't developed, and yes, accidents can happen, but I didn't do what he thought. I wasn't even home during the fire! But that neighbor was just so nosey and chatty, he'd talk to anyone who listened."

"So, what were you doing in your yard?"

I cleared my throat and scooped more gravy on the last biscuit. "I was playing with a little flower faerie. It was dusk, so her wings were lit up. I can see how it might look like I was playing with matches, but I wasn't. No idea where the fireballs came from."

He snickered and dunked a fry into his tuna melt. "You'd be surprised at the stuff a police officer hears from a hysterical witness. Once, I had an old lady swear that the Easter Bunny was breaking into her house every night." I laughed and noticed his smile.

Like he was relieved, I was laughing and not sad. "What was it?"

"It was a man with a mop of white hair. Turns out she wasn't wearing her glasses when this happened, and all that white hair turned into a rabbit in her mind." I snuck a fry off his plate and used it to get at the rest of the gravy on the plate.

"See, usually by the time I'm called, it actually *is* a giant rabbit."

Moss laughed. "Well, if I hear anyone disparaging you, I'll give them a piece of my mind. There's no way you were responsible for that fire."

I couldn't help but smile. It was nice having a friend on my side for once. "Appreciate that." Moss reached for another fry but stopped before he put it in his mouth. "What's up?"

"I'm remembering something." He threw his fry onto his plate and pulled out his phone. I watched him hit a few buttons and what looked like links to something. "How much do you remember about the night Howard died?" he asked, reading something.

I sat back and thought. "Well, maybe not as

much as yesterday, but a fair bit. Why?"

He started scrolling up on his phone. "Do you remember what that creature said to us? In the cemetery?"

I thought back on that awful night. "I remember he said we couldn't stop him. There's a full moon once a month and plenty of hearts that our hearts might work. Hmm, I'm sure he said more."

Moss handed me his phone. "Read that." I took the phone and read what looked to be his statement from that night. It mentioned everything I mentioned, plus something that drained the blood from my face.

"Oh my god."

"It said, 'The Order brought us forth.'" He tapped the table with a finger when he said forth.

"It did, I remember now, holy shit." I looked up at him, "The Order summoned that thing. It's their fault that Howard is gone."

"I think it's time we check out the haunted mansion."

CHAPTER ELEVEN

Moss was right. I felt much better with food in my stomach. Even if it didn't get rid of the anxious feeling in my gut, the hunger pains were gone, and I felt more awake. We drove back to the Fell's house, and I waited by his car while Moss called Officer Hyde again about the backup. We had to be sneaky. We couldn't let Ryan know what was going on, so I crossed my fingers that he was distracted with other major-esque duties.

Moss walked back over to me and wiggled his phone in the air. "Okay, we got back up."

"Great. Let's go." We hopped in his car and sped towards the old mansion. "Just head all the way down Magnolia, until you hit a fork, then go right. You can't miss it." Moss nodded and headed towards Magnolia, which was only a block away. It was still going to take a while to get to the mansion. The Fell's house was on the opposite side of town. "So, who's our backup?"

"Hyde said that Dennis and Greggs are coming. If it's necessary, they'll call in more official backup. Ryan be damned." I nervously tapped on my lap, praying to whichever deity was listening that we'd just find Amelia and Jackson renovating the mansion. That their phones were dead, and the blood in their house and in the storage unit wasn't real blood, and they put their witchy room in storage for some other reason. But I knew that was wishful thinking. There's no mistaking the smell of blood, especially that much of it.

"So, tell me about this place? Is it big?" Moss asked.

"Yeah. I've only been out there once, when I was in high school. People wanted to see if it was haunted, so they asked 'the weird girl' to come with them. It's got three stories, but I'm not sure if there's a basement, we didn't look that long. There's lots of rooms and a grand staircase in the foyer. So, unless someone comes out to meet us, we might be looking for a bit."

"Gotcha. *Is* it haunted?" I didn't blame him for asking. Honestly, I wanted to know, too. That's why I went all those years ago.

"If it was, they hid from me while there. I didn't sense or see anything." It was surprisingly comforting speaking with someone about this. I kept so much to myself as a kid, and even though I was almost thirty,

I only spoke to Amelia and Jackson about these sorts of things. I did talk to Howard about the preternatural side of the town, but he never seemed that interested. He just wanted to know, for knowing's sake.

"So why didn't you stay in the house long?"

I snickered. "I may have done a little wind spell to knock stuff over and scare them. It didn't take much."

Moss laughed. "Well, I'm sure they deserved it."

"They did, trust me." Normally, talking about my childhood made me sad, but Moss seemed to know how to get the good from the bad. It was nice. "Did you ever do anything like that? Break into supposedly haunted houses?"

"No, no, no, nothing like that. I did my fair share of hanging around cemeteries and drinking cheap beer, though. My group mainly loitered, thinking we were badasses with our JNCO jeans and long ponytails." I laughed. I had completely forgotten about my bad choice in clothing back then.

"Damn, I miss JNCO jeans."

"No matter how much I pulled them up, the ends always got torn up," Moss said, "I wonder if that was part of their strategy. Oh, when the end of their jeans gets destroyed, they'll _have_ to buy new ones!"

"Little did they realize that teenagers didn't

give a shit and thought it made them look cool!" We laughed because we knew it was true.

Moss turned one more corner, and we saw the Eldred Mansion at the end of its long driveway. The amount of dark magic in the air smacked into me like a brick wall, and I threw my left arm over Moss's chest. He slammed on his brakes and looked over at me wide-eyed. "You all right?" I was trying desperately not to shake. I had felt plenty of dark magic in my life, and it was always unnerving. It made your skin crawl and burn, and sometimes you even heard whispers, but once you felt it, it would stop. Almost like an alarm, 'watch out, there's bad stuff here,' but this, it was unending. It felt like it was being drawn from elsewhere, filling up the mansion.

"There's a spell making things wrong here." My voice came out a whisper.

He reached up and held my arm. "Can you tell how wrong?" It was an interesting question, something I hadn't considered. How does one quantify 'wrong' in magic?

"I can't. It could be an echo of a spell or something happening now." I looked at Moss, and his attentive face gave me courage. "Keep going."

He nodded and gently tapped the gas as I finally took my arm back, and we started inching our way along the long driveway toward the huge house.

Halfway to the mansion, we came up to the large iron gate. Moss stopped, and we got out of his car. I shut the door and finally gave into the shivers the dark magic made me feel, and the feeling finally went away.

"Cold?" Moss replaced his regular bullets with the standard issue silver that every police officer gets, just in case.

"Scared." I pulled the little baggy of ashes out of my pocket and poured the last bit of them on the hood. I snapped my fingers, and the ashes flashed, one good ball of fire which let me inhale just enough smoke to get my spell to work. I thought about Amelia and Jackson. I wanted to find them, alive or not, and I breathed out the smoke.

Moss walked over with a little smile on his face. "Makes you look like a dragon."

I chuckled. "That's why I like that spell." The smoke curled in the air for a minute before turning into a straight line that moved towards the mansion. "Let's follow it." Moss kept his sidearm pointed at the ground, but I knew he was ready for anything. We walked up to the giant iron gate and saw it was locked with a chain and a huge padlock on the other side. But this lock didn't have a keyhole.

"Well, I'm good but not *that* good," Moss said. "What do we do about that?"

"We unlock it silly." My hand hovered over

the chain, I wouldn't be caught off guard by another spell, so I had to check everything. Thankfully, I didn't detect a spell on it, so I grabbed the chain, "*Patefacio,*" and watched the chain and the now open lock spill to the ground.

"What does Patefacio mean?" Moss asked quietly.

I looked over at him and shrugged. "Open."

He looked surprised, and I suppressed a chuckle. "That easy, huh?"

"Depends on the spell and the witch. Which trigger you choose can make things more difficult, too. You know how I snap my fingers for fire?" He nodded. "Well, I tried using 'fuego' for fire when I first started, and let's just say after one weekend at a Bomba Estereo concert, I changed that really quick."

"Why's that?" he asked with a smirk that made one of his dimples show.

I turned to him, my arms crossed over my stomach. "'Fuego' is a well-known song from their album 'Blow Up,' and it's said no less than thirty times in the song. When I sang along, I...unintentionally started a bunch of fires. They figured it was just a crazed fan, so I wasn't caught, but no one was hurt! If they were, I would have turned myself in."

He snickered and shook his head. "Remind me never to invite you to jazz brunch," he said, snapping his fingers like a beatnik.

"Oh my god." I playfully slapped his arm and pushed the gate open. "Like I'd ever go to jazz brunch." We stepped through the gate, and the abandoned mansion loomed before us.

It was your usual three-story renaissance-style mansion built in a small town where it didn't match the rest of the houses. The once glistening white paint was now gray and peeling off in huge chunks. The beautiful vines that once only wound around the columns had taken over the entire building. You could see where they went into the house through broken windows that no one fixed. I didn't see anyone on the grounds or in the house from where we were. I looked to my right and saw the gray smoke twitching, begging me to follow it. "This way," I said quietly and followed.

We walked through the dying, overgrown grass and vines towards the north side of the yard. The fence was lined with white oleander trees. No one had pruned them back in twenty years, so they were huge white clouds that grew into each other. Since it was finally turning into fall, there were a bunch of white flowers already littering the ground.

"Pretty," Moss said quietly.

"Yeah, poisonous, too. Apparently, even eating honey that bees made after pollinating white oleander can hurt you."

"Dang, now I'm off honey." Our steps were muted thanks to the thick grass and flower petals under our feet. Which was good because I am not a sneaky person. We followed the smoke around the trees, and I watched it glide through a dilapidated wooden fence.

After a few more steps, it hit us. "Ugh, oh my god." The smell of rotting flesh made us both gag and cover our mouths with our shirts. Fat lot of good that would do, but it was instinctual. "Oh shit." I groaned and pushed on the wooden gate. There was resistance, but with a good shove, it opened a few inches. Moss stepped in front of me, and I let him. He was the police officer, after all. He was able to open the gate wider, and a weird squelching noise made my ears twitch. Moss had pushed the fence through a huge person-shaped green blob. It was wearing a familiar shirt, and I felt my heart drop into my feet. "That's Jackson's shirt," I whispered, my lower lip slightly quivering. It was hard to forget a red plaid shirt with dancing elves on it. He wore it no matter the season.

"What the hell?" Moss whispered. We could see a huge chunk missing from what I suspect was its head. Perhaps this was where our lovely green blob came from? "How on earth did he turn into goo?"

I shook my head. "I don't know, but I know it can't be good." Moss sighed and stepped around the goo and into the backyard. I saw him jerk a second before his shoulders lowered. "I think we found Amelia." He motioned for me to join him, and I did. I don't imagine much could make a detective jerk in surprise, so I braced myself. I stepped around Jackson's gooey body and saw Amelia on the ground, absolutely covered in blood. She was wearing the same clothes I saw her in the day before, so it was easy to identify her. But her face, it had been smashed in so violently it was gone. I saw her legs seemed to be missing from the hips down, but the leaves and dead petals on the ground were covered in a familiar green goo. "They were killed then...turned into goo?" Nothing about this made sense.

"I guess Nicola nailed it by testing the blood type," Moss said. "Still doesn't tell us what happened, though." I shook my head, agreeing with him. I looked at my friends, both murdered and tossed out like trash. I could feel angry, hot tears at the corner of my eyes, but I blinked furiously to keep them back.

"Wasn't supposed to be another friend." Moss laid his hand on my shoulder, and I welcomed the touch. I needed something to ground me as I stared at the bodies of my friends. "Whoever did this to them is dead," I whispered.

"Let's go back to the car and radio for more help. There are bodies here, we need the medical examiner, and now we have probable cause to go inside without a warrant." I nodded and followed him back through the oleander. It was less pretty this time.

We got back to his car, and he got on the radio. Now that we had found the bodies, there was no need to hide from Ryan. Honestly, I half wanted him to come at me yelling about wasting resources for this. He'd go home with a frog for a nose if he did. "Dispatch, this is Detective Moss, I'm with Roa, and we need backup at the Eldred Mansion. We have two dead bodies, so we need the M.E. The bodies are identified as Jackson and Amelia Fell."

The radio crackled. "Dispatch, we read you. Backup is on the way." It clicked one more time.

"Moss, this is D and G. We're close. We'll be there soon." We knew they'd be close, and I was glad about that.

"Copy that," he said and put the receiver back on the dash.

"D and G? That Dennis and Greggs?" I asked, leaning against the car.

"Yeah, they're trying a thing, I think." He shook his head. "It's not working."

I chuckled. "Least they're having fun." I sighed and stared at the ground, willing the tears back into my eyes.

Moss stepped in front of me and laid a hand on my shoulder. "Let me know if you need to back off."

I shook my head and swallowed hard. "I won't,"
I looked up at him, "personality flaw."

"Is that your only flaw?"

"Ha! I have many flaws." Moss met my eyes,
and I saw those little brown specks get bigger. "If you
stick around long enough, you just may learn them
all."

He smiled. "I'm not going anywhere." I reached
up and laid my hand on his, and his fingers tangled
with mine, and it hit me. It had been a long time since I
had touched anyone like this. It wasn't a friendly hug,
or a nice to meet you handshake. It was something just
for us, something that was just a bit more than friendly.

I heard sirens for a moment and saw another
police car driving up the road. Moss took his hand
back, and I let him. No need for rumors to fly. The
sirens turned off, and they pulled up behind Moss's
car and quickly got out.

"G and D, I presume?"

"D and G." The one with Dennis on his name
tag said, correcting me.

I looked over at Moss. "Wow, they do take that
seriously, don't they?" He tried to cover a laugh with
a cough, but I could tell the duo of D and G didn't
appreciate the tease. Seems D, Dennis, was the older of
the two. Taller than Moss by a few inches with a bushy
brown mustache. G, Greggs, was young, clean-shaven,

and his shirt seemed a little baggy.

"We waiting or going in now?" Dennis asked. I pushed off the car and turned to Moss. This was more his area than mine.

"I think we need to go in now, see if anyone is here," he said. "If we find anyone, they're suspects in the death of Jackson and Amelia Fell."

The other two police officers visibly sank. "Can't believe this. I liked Jackson." Greggs said.

"Me too.," Dennis agreed, "No matter what the Major said, they were good people." All three of them made sure to load their guns with silver bullets just in case. Those were good for about everything in the preternatural world. Moss gave me a nod and held his gun in both hands, pointing it at the ground.

"Let's go say hi."

"Nice." I winked at him and started for the gate.

He chuckled. "Not too much?"

"Nope, perfect." I pushed the gate open wider, and it made a loud screech. That was fine, I was mad, and I didn't feel like being sneaky anymore. We got to the door, and I let the police officers do what they were trained for.

"Go ahead and knock, just in case," Moss suggested.

Dennis nodded and knocked on the door with a fist. "Arion Police Department, open up!" he yelled.

It was a good police voice, stern without being overly confrontational. He knocked three more times with no response. "Guess we're letting ourselves in." As he raised his leg to kick the door, I felt energy building behind it. It's always hard to describe. My fingers start tingling, and the feeling moves up my arm and makes me shiver.

I reached out to grab his arm. "Wait, Dennis, no!" But I was too slow. His leg hadn't even kicked the door before it splintered into a million pieces. The force of a fireball knocked all of us on our butts, and we landed a few feet away from the porch. My head hit the ground, and my ears started ringing. I could hear muffled yelling around me.

Moss appeared above me. He looked worried. "Are you all right?" His lips formed.

I nodded even though I knew I was hurt. We could deal with that later. "Yeah, help me up." I held out my hand, and he pulled me to sitting. I saw Dennis on the ground a few feet away. Greggs was pulling large chunks of the door out of his partner's arm and putting a tourniquet above the wound.

I held out my hand. "*Exsarcio!*" My ears popped, and I shook my head as my hearing returned. Greggs and Moss did the same, but Dennis would need more than I could do for him. Thank God backup was on the way.

Greggs got on the radio on his shoulder. "Officer down! We need an ambulance now!" His radio crackled, but nothing came through except garbled speech.

"Backup's coming, Greggs, don't worry," I said. But it didn't matter what I said. His partner was incapacitated, and police officers took that hard. I never blame them. They go through a lot together, and now Greggs had to go through this awful house without his partner.

"Come on, let's get these bastards." Moss helped me to my feet, and I held my hand out in front of me. This time, the police officers walked behind me as we stepped inside. I cast a spell that would cover the three of us. "*Clipeum.*" It would be able to deflect objects and a few spells, fireball included.

It was dark inside the mansion. Late afternoon autumn light streamed through the trees and broken windows, so the light was sparse. The room wasn't as large as I remember it, but that's how it goes, I guess. I was a teenager the last time I was here. The large staircase that peeled off in two different directions was about a hundred feet in front of us, but so far, we hadn't seen anyone. No matter how quietly we tried to move, our footsteps echoed off the marble floor. Greggs and Moss left the safety of my spell and started searching around the room. There were a few large crates to our left, but no one behind them.

"Ugh, smells familiar." Moss wrinkled his nose. I closed my eyes and let my tingly fingers detect magic. There were five individuals through a door that was below the staircase that went up to my right. There was one in a room that was off the entryway, along with another kind of magic that made me shiver. It felt wrong, like death magic, cold and empty. Just another unpleasant surprise. It was seven against three. I suppose it could have been worse. I tapped my foot twice, and Moss turned to me. I held up five fingers and pointed to the door under the stairs, then two fingers and pointed to the far door. He nodded and moved to Greggs, who had started up the stairs.

"G," he whispered. But Greggs didn't hear him, and he took another step up the stairs.

"Greggs, stop," I whispered, but it was too late. He took one more step up the stairs, and my ear twitched as it heard a click. Greggs looked at me for a second before an explosion sent him flying back into me. My shield was useless, it being for small debris and magic. A man flying into me was something I hadn't considered. We both went flying backwards, landing hard against the marble floor, sliding towards the open door. Greggs was a thin man, but with all the equipment, guns, clips, and bulletproof vest, he was a good thirty pounds heavier. I managed to roll him off me and saw his face and chest were burned. "Greggs, are you okay?" But he didn't answer.

Moss slid next to us, and I felt his hands on my back. "You all right?"

"Yeah, but G's down too." Moss quickly picked up the unconscious police officer and put him outside with his partner, leaving me inside. I got to my feet as the five casters spilled from the back room. In bad guy cliché fashion, they were wearing black robes. "Really? Nobody wanted to wear a yellow robe? Purple?" They ignored my witty remark as they formed a half-circle in front of me.

"Lily Roa," A woman in front of me said, and I jerked in shock. How did she know my name? "You are a talented witch. The Order is interested in your power. Cooperate, and we will spare you."

I rolled my eyes. *Screw this bitch* I thought. "Oh yeah? Did you tell that to Jackson or Amelia? Because they were just as talented as me, more so, and they didn't deserve to die!" I roared at her.

"He was poking around," another of them said, a young man. "We didn't want him, and he wouldn't leave. He said he would expose us, and obviously, we couldn't have that. His wife followed soon after."

I stared at him, and if my eyes could throw daggers, they would have. "Didn't want him? Even if you 'didn't want him,' you didn't have to kill them! And turning them into goo? What the hell kind of spell is that!" My fists were shaking at my side. I was so angry and scared. I had never faced off against so many foes at once. And this wasn't even all of them.

A chuckle spilled from behind the duo. "You'd have to ask our Master about that. Quite an ingenious way to get rid of the evidence, isn't it?"

"Arion police hands up!" Moss yelled as he ran inside, pointing his gun at the group. "You're all under arrest! Sit on the ground and put your hands on your head!" I was relieved Moss had come back in, but I also knew they didn't care if he was a cop or not. He stopped next to me, his gun still pointing at them. "Down now!" The group chuckled and pointed at us. I quickly put up my shield spell as five spells hit it at once. I could feel my shield crack as my feet slid back a few inches. All their spells together were too much for my shield.

"Moss, run!" I grabbed him and took cover behind the large crates. Spells were going off all around us, and chunks of the floor and nearby wall were exploding in our faces. I could smell blood wafting out of the crates, and I didn't want to think what disgusting thing the Order had put inside them. Moss kept peeking around the corners, but every time he did, a spell would splinter a little bit of the crate.

"Kinda young for an Order," Moss said, ducking from flying debris.

"They mentioned a Master. That's probably the one in that room over there, not joining in the fight like evil people in charge tend to do."

The woman who spoke earlier yelled out, "I suppose the goo wasn't the most dignified death we could have given your friends! Let's go for more... culturally appropriate for *you*, shall we?"

"Culturally appropriate? What the hell does that mean?" Moss asked.

I looked up and saw flames licking the ceiling. "They want to burn us to death." I could feel the heat of the fire surrounding us. It was moving quickly. I had no doubt it was being helped along.

"Any ideas?" Moss yelled over the noise. Truthfully, I had an idea, but it was crazy. But I suppose when dealing with a crazy cult, that's the kind of plan you need.

"So, I take it you like dragons?" I asked.

He turned, confused, which I expected. "Dragons? Are you going to do that spell again?"

I shook my head and made a mental note of where in the room the cultists were. "Not exactly." I turned back to him and grabbed his shirt. "Whatever you hear, don't come out until I say so, okay?"

Worry spread on his face. "What are you going to do?"

"Kill a couple birds with their own fire." I

started to turn, but before I could let go of his shirt, I felt his hands around my wrists.

"Lily, wait." I turned back to him as he pulled me close and kissed me. It was an 'Oh shit, we're gonna die, I better get that kiss' kind of kisses. I'd never had one before, but you know it when it happens. The pressure was perfect, the amount of tongue was ideal, it was like we'd done it a million times before. I don't know if I recommend them cause of the possibility of dying and all, but man, was it good.

When he pulled away, I finally let go of his shirt. "Damn, boy. Stay here!" I glimpsed his smile before I rounded the corner and got to my feet. I held my left hand out and focused on the spell that was making the fire worse. It was weaving around the fire, pure force, and my entire arm started vibrating slightly. Everything felt like it was going in slow motion. I needed that fire the spell was making worse, I needed that spell. That fire was mine, and it had to do what I wanted!

I breathed in deep, pushing all my power, will, and intention into my own spell, and yelled. "*Mine!*" I needed that spell. I needed it to save Moss and G and D. I needed it to save any firefighters the burden of putting it out and possibly getting hurt. I needed it to avenge my friends! I yelled until I felt the spell pull from the fire and wrap around my arm. That pure magical force swirled around my arm, and I lifted my hand to the flame-covered ceiling. The fire easily recognized that spell and abandoned the original wielder and became mine. The foyer slowly dimmed as I drew the fire into myself. It flowed into my outstretched left arm and then ignited my right arm. It was mine now. I was its master. It would listen to no one but me. If Moss liked dragons, I'd show him one.

Another cultist popped out from behind the stairwell, confused as to where the fire went, and I pointed my fiery right arm at them and launched a basketball-sized fireball in their direction. He couldn't get out of the way in time, and his scream echoed in the marble room. I heard a shift to my right and turned to see another cultist. It was the woman who was mocking me earlier. She had short blonde hair and seemed to abandon her magic for a gun that she was pointing at me.

"What's the matter?" I couldn't help myself. I had to goad her. "Don't believe in your own magic?" Not only was my arm covered in fire, but my voice had a distinct crackle to it now.

"You think you can…" I didn't bother waiting to see what she was going to say and launched another fireball at her. I cringed at the sound of her skull smacking into the marble floor. When will bad guys learn we don't care what they have to say?

"Lily, look out!" Moss yelled, and I turned back to him. He was standing up, doing the exact opposite of what I told him to do! His gun was pointed at the stairs, but before he pulled the trigger, pain shocked through my right shoulder, and the fire surrounding my arm retreated into my body. I fell to the floor as Moss's gun went off, and I heard another thud behind me. I looked over and saw a third cultist on the ground, a perfect red hole in his forehead. Moss ran over to me, his gun still raised. "Can you move?" He halfway picked me up with my good shoulder and dragged me back behind the large crates. There were still two more cultists out there, but it was quiet. I had no idea where they were, and the pain was keeping me from concentrating. Moss took my ruined jacket off. "Let me see." I saw a nasty round wound just above my shoulder bone as blood poured down my arm.

"My arm feels numb and tingly asleep at the same time." My voice was shaky, I assume, from the adrenaline wearing off.

"Here, can you move your hand?" He laid my hand in his, and I was able to move my fingers and push on his hand a little, but that part hurt. "Okay, I don't think anything's broken. You'll have a nasty scar, though."

"Sexy." I groaned and laid my other hand on my wound, and closed my eyes. Despite the pain, I pushed my magic into my arm, picturing the wound slowly stitching itself closed. But it was difficult. Images of where the other cultists might be kept creeping into my thoughts, and I was so worried that our backup still hadn't arrived that I knew it wasn't going to be a nice clean scar. But I didn't care. I just wanted to stop bleeding. I moved my hand and saw the wound was no longer bleeding, but it did indeed look bad. Instead of a nice, round scar, my skin looked lumped together like a toddler made a lake out of Play-Doh.

"I thought it would look better," Moss said.

I shook my head. "I couldn't concentrate enough." I looked up at him. "Why didn't you stay hidden?"

"I had to see what was going on, and when I saw that guy on the stairs, I couldn't do nothing. He had you in his sights."

I huffed. "If you die, I'm gonna raise you just so I can kill you again."

He smirked. "Deal." I riffled through my jacket pockets and found the two vials I had from my apartment and shoved them in my pants pockets. He helped me to my feet, and I only felt a little woozy. We walked around the big crates and saw the last two cultists slowly standing from around the stairs, their hands up over their heads. Guess they didn't want to fight. Moss quickly handcuffed them to the banister, their arms behind their backs. I reached into my pockets and pulled out one of the vials.

"Just wait here, you two," I said and smashed it on the ground next to them and watched as their heads lolled to the side.

"What was that?" Moss asked.

"Can't cast if they're not awake." I turned to the doors that hid the last two cultists. It hadn't opened during the entire fight. "There's two in there."

"Ready for a boss fight?" Moss asked.

I smiled at him. "I bet we'll level up after this one."

"Hell, I bet we get two levels." I laughed and pooled the last of the fire inside me, and launched the biggest fireball I could at the door. The door exploded in splinters, and I recalled my shield spell for the both of us. Splinters flew around us, bouncing off my shield, and when the noise stopped, I looked in the room. There was only one person in the room. An old man standing by the blazing fireplace. *Why did I sense two?* I wondered. I looked around for more cultists and felt for more magic, but all I saw was the old man and a mundane suit of armor. It wasn't where I had sensed the magic earlier, and nothing was emanating from it. I wondered if someone had escaped, but we'd have to deal with that later.

"Ah, there you are." The old man snapped his

fingers, and Moss crumpled to the ground like a rag doll.

"Richard!" I kneeled next to him and felt a pulse at his neck. He was asleep.

"You put my help to sleep," the old man said, "it's only fair I do the same to yours." I stood back up and faced him. He was short and bald. His black dress pants looked pressed, and his black suspenders stood out against his white shirt. I, of course, had no idea who he was. "Please, Ms. Roa, have a seat." He waved his hand, and a chair in the room moved to face me.

"I'll stand, thanks." I walked into the room, and I could feel the sneer on my lips. The heavy scent of incense hit my nose, but it did nothing to hide the sickening, sweet smell of death. "Did you kill Jackson and Amelia? Did you turn them into goo!"

He sighed and took a seat in a chair across from me. "I did, yes. He knew we were here and wanted to expose us. His wife found out that he discovered us, so we brought her here. We could always use a talented medium like her, but—" he shrugged his shoulders. "She refused. So, I had to get rid of her too."

My lower lip quivered a bit. "They didn't deserve to die like that! They were the only…" I stopped myself, I was getting hysterical, and that wouldn't help me here.

"They were what?" the old man laid an ankle

on his knee. "The only other witches here?" I froze at his words. "I know this little town doesn't appreciate you either."

"You're the Order of the Elements, aren't you?"

He smiled, his sparkling white teeth gleaming. "We are, yes. I knew you'd figure it out."

I took a step towards him. "How long have you been here?" I was surprised I was able to keep my voice from wavering.

"About eight months. You're impressive. Not many witches can take on a Sluagh and live to tell the tale."

"Truthfully, it was a revenge seeking Elf that did the deed. Why don't you go find him instead?"

He chuckled. "I know, but still. I had to assess you." I really didn't care what he had to say. I just wanted to keep him talking until backup got here. They should have been here by now! "Do you know what we do?" he asked, as if I gave a damn.

I shrugged. "Kill innocent people like a bunch of assholes?"

He waved me off. "Besides that." I stood with my feet shoulder-width apart, trying to ground myself, to try to help my magic react quicker, but something in the room threw me off. It felt like the big black blob in the precinct. It all made sense now.

"You create chaos in peaceful towns for no

reason!"

He smiled and gave a little chuckle. "We find talent. And we use that talent to unleash power into the world that was once asleep. We're extremely selective of our members, and you've made quite a dent in our membership in less than an hour. I'm impressed."

"Screw you." I really wanted to be more creative, but I was still weak from blood loss. My snark tank was running low.

He laughed. "Yes, yes, screw me all that. Now," he got to his feet. "The Order of the Elements could use you."

I felt the world around me spinning. "You did not just ask me to join the evil organization that killed three of my friends in less than a month."

He smiled as he walked around to the back of his chair. "I did, actually."

I scoffed. "You're insane."

"Just a bit." he winked at me. "Imagine the knowledge you could gain with our association." He motioned to the room, and I realized we were in a library. Every twelve-foot-high shelf was filled with books, and I won't lie. I wanted to read every single one of them. Knowledge is power, after all. "You, Miss Roa, could make everyone in this provincial town sorry they ever said a bad word against you." His attitude was pissing me off. Yes, it was provincial, and yes, everyone hated me, but I still loved my town. It didn't deserve to be razed to the ground or destroyed by a sleeping tentacled God or whatever they wanted to wake up this time.

I raised my right arm, but with a mere look, he managed to push it behind my back. I yelled as the new skin on my wound began to tear. "Well, if you don't want to join." My arm twisted against my will, and I screamed as the wound tore completely open. I could feel blood pouring down my arm again.

"Let her go!" I gasped and turned as far as I could and saw Moss standing in the doorway, gun in one hand, pointing it at the old man. The other was holding onto the door frame. He looked like he was still fighting against the sleep spell. "Let her go, or so help me, I'll shoot you dead!"

"Do you think you can shoot me before I think about breaking her neck?" he said. Moss didn't bother to answer. He fired his silver-loaded gun at the old man, but instead of hitting him or anything in the room, Moss yelled out, and I watched him fall back to the floor.

"Richard!"

"He needn't bother with that gun," the old man said dismissively. "He'd never be able to hurt me with it anyway." I turned back to the old man, and I felt my eyes turn red. The gall, the audacity of this man! How dare he hurt my partner! I raised my left arm. Spells from my dominant hand were more powerful, but it was out of commission for the moment, and I couldn't just do nothing. I had to try.

"*Suffocant!*" The old man grabbed his throat, and I felt the spell holding my hurt arm dissipate. It fell limply against my side, and I didn't want to move again, but I needed it. Screaming in pain and rage, I raised my right hand to meet the other. The screaming helps, trust me. I focused on my spell, gathering power, and squeezed harder. His little bald head was turning purple. *Almost, almost,* I said to myself. He took a hand from his throat and pointed at me, but there was no way he could concentrate enough to cast anything.

A noise clinked to my right, and my ear twitched, but I turned too late. The suit of armor was rushing towards me, sword raised. I saw yellow eyes in the helmet. It was a revenant, hiding in plain sight! He put a poor dead body in that suit to protect him, and I fell for it. I managed to perceive it a second before the sword it held sliced through the air and through my shoulder. The sword must have been extremely sharp because I barely felt any pain as my right arm fell with a thump to the wooden floor.

Explosions went off around me, and the revenant fell to the ground. I couldn't tell who or what was causing the explosions. I just cared that they didn't hurt me. There was more yelling and running footsteps as I fell to my knees. I looked up from my severed arm and saw my left arm still gesturing to the old man, still choking him. Everything was happening so slowly it felt like an eternity. I screamed and squeezed my left hand closed. The man's head jerked to the side, and his body fell lifelessly onto the carpet.

My energy drained so quickly that I fell to the carpet without a care in the world. There were more people running around and yelling, but no more explosions. 'Roa! Roa!' It sounded like someone was calling me, but I couldn't tell who. A blurry image appeared above me.

"Roa!" Slowly, the person came into focus. It was Major Ryan.

"Hurry, get her to the ambulance!" someone yelled.

"You're going to be all right." I felt pressure against my shoulder, but it didn't hurt. I think that was bad. *Shouldn't that hurt?* I thought.

"Why are you being nice?" I asked, or I think I asked. At that point, I might have only thought of the words. I could feel hands under me, picking me up.

"You're going to be all right." Ryan carried me from the room, and everything went dark.

CHAPTER TWELVE

I heard a steady beeping, and it kept me from falling back asleep. I was alive and…so _high_ holy crap. I felt like I was floating, and I felt myself smile at nothing and hoped I wouldn't start giggling. I opened my eyes and saw Moss sitting next to the bed.

He smiled. "Welcome back." He looked good as usual. His left arm was in a large sling and immobile. But he was wearing clothes, not hospital attire. How long had I been out?

"What happened to you?" I managed to ask. I smacked my lips a few times. I needed a drink in the worst way.

"Seems my bullet bounced back at me when I tried to shoot the old man. Got me in the bicep." He filled up a little cup with some water from a nearby pitcher and helped navigate a straw into my mouth. I took a few long swings until my mouth no longer felt like it was full of cotton.

"Ahh. Man, that's rough." My mind was swimming. Hell, so was everything else. "Is this morphine? Damn." I had never had any kind of painkiller besides Advil, so this was an interesting experience.

He chuckled. "Yeah. It took two surgeries, about twelve hours each, to re-attach your arm. They were worried they were doing it for nothing, but I told them you'd be able to fix what they couldn't." He set the cup on a nearby tray and tried to fluff the pillow under my head. "That was a week ago."

The wonderful smell of his cologne woke me up a little more. "Surgery? A week?"

"Yeah. Do you remember what happened?" I looked over at my right arm. It was bandaged from my neck to my hand and immobile in a suspended sling.

"Oh yeah, that old asshole tore it off. Or a sword, or…something."

"You don't seem put out at that." He sounded surprised. I looked back over at him with a smile that I hoped didn't make me look too ridiculous.

"Meh, I'm too high to care about much. Besides," I wiggled my left hand. "Magic, remember? I'll fine, I mean…I'll be fine. Just like you said."

"Good. I'd hate to lose you as a partner."

"Phbt, you're not going to lose me that easy.

Did we get them?" The way he shifted in his chair told me he had unwelcome news. It couldn't be all bad. I know the leader was dead.

"The two we had in custody from the mansion committed suicide."

"What?" That news killed my buzz just a little. "How did that happen?"

"They had cyanide caplets in their teeth. Real old-fashioned World War II spy shit. No one was expecting it. The one we got in your apartment, well..."

"What? Just an average magically inclined burglar?"

Moss sighed. I could hear he was irritated. "When Kyle and Mo took him to the precinct, Ryan noticed they were trying to put him in the anti-magic cell."

"Oh no."

He nodded. "Made them put him in a regular cell, didn't believe them when they told him he was invisible in your apartment. An hour later, he was gone. Never got prints or a name."

I sighed. "Freaking perfect. So, we know who killed Jackson and Amelia but don't know why they were here, other than me, I guess." Anger was starting to kill my buzz. How could Ryan have done that?

"For the moment, anyway. We have every available police officer going over that house, looking for anything. We found a bunch of books, and after going through about a dozen of them, we found a spell that dissolved the dead."

"Let me guess, into goo?"

"That's our guess. From what we could tell from the Fell's books that were in the storage unit, Jackson had been studying the Order for years. When he began to suspect the Order was here, he wanted to get rid of them. Seems the Order found him snooping around, and with Amelia's affinity for the dead..."

"She found Jackson before we did." I shook my head, trying to hold back tears. "What an awful way to find out your husband is dead. I guess it *was* him trying to contact me." I might have to try to contact them when I get home. Whenever that would be. Tell them I'm sorry I couldn't help them.

"I suggested when it's no longer needed as evidence, you could have the contents of that storage unit."

"What a crappy way to stock my room." I closed my eyes. "Damn it. I shouldn't have killed the old man."

"He would have killed you. You didn't have a choice. We'll figure this out. I have a feeling this won't be the last time we hear about this Order."

"Dun-dun-dun." I sang slowly. "How are Dreggs and Gennis" Moss snickered, and I knew the morphine was kicking in again. "Wait…that's not right." He laughed, and I remembered how much I liked to make him laugh.

"D and G? They're fine. Dennis had a mild concussion, and a few abrasions, one bad puncture, and Greggs had a few small skin grafts done. He'll be released soon. The others found the remains of Jackson and Amelia. Nicola was able to get them back together and cremate them per their wishes. After she went over them with a fine-tooth comb, that is. She had a theory about how Jackson's head goo got into town. After Amelia was found half turned into goo, Nicola thought that the spell might take a while to 'kick in,' and a big bird of prey found the body, and well, depending on how he was killed, it could have picked up the head while it was still a head."

"And when it turned to goo, it slipped through its talons and fell back to Earth. That could account for those slashes in it. How weird, and that's saying something." Moss laid a hand on my left arm. It was warm and alerted me to how cold I was, even under the blanket.

"When Nicola learned the reason for the bodies turning into goo was in one of the spell books, she decided to defer to you on the research as to the how."

"Yes, goo is bad." Man, it was hard to think with all these drugs. Familiar clacking heels walked into the room, and I saw Nicola come in. She was put together as always in a dark purple dress suit. I had a feeling she was visiting before going to work.

"Hello there, feeling better?" she asked and sat on the bed across from Moss.

"Yes, Mary Poppins." I tried my best cockney accent, but the drugs were interfering.

She snorted and shook her head. "Morphine?"

Moss smiled. "Quite a bit of it, I think."

"Did you hear my arm fell off?" I asked her.

Nicola flashed that perfect smile of hers. "I did. You going to magic it back on?"

"Naw, the docs did that, I'll magic it better. Be fine." I was having trouble remembering what happened at the house, but not what happened before. "Oh no! Our night out."

Nicola chuckled. "It's all right. When you can drink again, I'm going to take you to New Orleans to celebrate. So, no getting your other arm chopped off, okay?"

"Deal," I said with a smile. I turned back to Moss, I shouldn't have been trying to remember everything that happened, but I'm stubborn. Moss and I were hiding behind boxes, and things were exploding around us, but other bits were still fuzzy.

"Starting to remember?" Nicola rubbed my leg.

"A little. Hiding behind boxes and...a dragon?

That doesn't sound right. What do you remember?"

Moss just shrugged. "Not much. I remember smoke and getting shot and boxes exploding. Now that you mention the boxes, I remember hiding behind them. I think that's when you talked about the dragon." His thumb ran gently along my good arm. "I'll let the nurses know you're awake." As I watched him leave the room, a memory was dangling in front of me. My brain really wanted me to remember. Suddenly, remembering him saying 'dragon' made something click. We were hiding behind the boxes, and I told him not to move, and then...I gasped as it hit me. The 'oh shit, we're gonna die kiss.'

Nicola leaned closer. "What is it?"

"Oh my god, Nicola!" I motioned for her to get even closer, and she did. "He kissed me!" I whispered. At least, I hope I was whispering. It was a little hard to control the volume of my voice on these drugs.

Nicola gasped and sat back. "Really? When? How was it?" The memory of the kiss made the beeping in the room faster. We both looked over at the machine and laughed.

"In the mansion, before we got hurt, it was amazing, but I don't think he remembers!"

"Oh no!" she chuckled. "Well, you could ask, I suppose."

"Yeah, you know, when I'm not high as a kite

and maybe when I can move my arm again."

She clicked her tongue. "Whatever you think is best. I won't push." she got to her feet. "Let me know when they'll release you, I can come pick you up."

"Thank you, mate." The morphine was really making my fake British accent awesome.

Nicola scoffed. "That's terrible, and you know it. I'll see you later." She patted my leg and left me alone. I closed my eyes and tried to remember more, but nothing came to mind.

"Lily?" I opened my eyes, and Moss was peeking around the curtain. "Um, there's someone here to see you, but I wasn't too sure if you'd want to see him."

"Who is it?"

"It's…Major Ryan." I felt my eyes try to pop out of my head. What the hell did he want?

"He does know I'm on lots of drugs and can't be held accountable for what I say and how loud I say it to him, right?"

"I do." Ryan's voice floated around the curtain a moment before he walked next to Moss. "I wanted to apologize, Roa." He was in his dress blues. Usually reserved for special occasions. Visiting injured police officers in the hospital was one of those occasions, and I was touched by the gesture.

"Oh? For what exactly?" I had to hear it from him that he realized just how wrong he was about this whole thing.

He sighed, twirling his hat in his hands. "For not treating you witches with the respect you deserve."

"You think maybe if you had, we could have saved Amelia? We might have one less body to bury, the one alive suspect wouldn't have gotten away, and I wouldn't be the only witch in this small ass town who already hates me?"

He nodded. "I do. I...don't know what I was thinking. I guess, in a way, I thought you were invulnerable. That Jackson and Amelia weren't in trouble, and it was a waste to look. But Roa, when I saw you on that floor, your arm...and you were still going. It was the bravest thing I've ever seen. So, I'm sorry, Ms. Roa. The Chief let the town know in a press conference that you were responsible for getting rid of a group of dangerous magic users and that your actions were selfless and brave. Hopefully, the town will start to lay off you." He was quiet for a moment. He was never quiet. His eyes weren't full of hate and annoyance. They were sad and apologetic. Even on the drugs, I could tell he meant it.

"Thank you." He nodded and left the room.

"Well, I wasn't sure what he was going to say." Moss sat on the end of the bed. "But I could tell he felt bad for what happened."

"He should. Maybe he won't yell at me so much

anymore?"

He shrugged with his free shoulder. "Anything's possible."

"So, uh," I sucked on my bottom lip and realized I was in desperate need of Chapstick. "If you remember more, let me know?"

He smiled. "Absolutely."

"Like…anything at all, okay?"

Moss laughed. "Yeah, anything at all."

I sighed and closed my eyes. "Awesome."

I felt his lips on my forehead. "It was awesome, wasn't it?"

My eyes flew open, and I scoffed. "You do remember! Jackass."

He laughed, and it made me smile. "How could I not? It was a 'we're about to die' kiss."

"That's exactly what I was thinking!" He stood up and hung his jacket off his good arm. "You're not leaving, are you?"

"You get more rest. I'll be by tomorrow. Shall I bring breakfast?"

I smiled. "Pancakes, please."

"As you wish." He gave me a soft kiss on my lips and walked out of the room. I chuckled and wondered how long it was going to take to get my arm working. I reached over with my left hand and touched the right side of my collarbone. Even high on morphine, I could push a little healing magic into my arm, and I watched the fingers on my right hand slowly curl. "Excellent."

Karen Thrower was born in Tulsa, OK, and still resides there with her husband, daughter, and cat. She graduated from The University of Tulsa with a BA in Deaf Education in 2005. She is a member of Oklahoma Science Fiction Writers and has served in several capacities, such as President, VP, and is currently Facebook Wizard. She has been published in various genres since 2018 and was included in the bestselling anthology 'Secret Stairs: A Tribute to Urban Legend' in 2019.